THE STRANGER

It was a person, a boy, standing by the rail, head bowed as if he were looking down at the water. His back was to her, so she couldn't recognize him. How strange that someone else could be out here. Her heart skipped a beat. Maybe it was one of the rebels. So what if it is, she told herself. They're just your former classmates.

She moved closer. Then called out tentatively, "Hello?"

She must have taken him by surprise, because despite the fact that he was taller and bigger than she was, he fell back onto the bridge. Face to face, she saw immediately that he wasn't one of the rebels. He wasn't a member of the Community either. He was no one she'd ever seen before in her life.

He gazed at her vaguely, with the lightest, bluest eyes he'd ever seen. His face was handsome, in a movie-star way—square jaw, straight nose, no blemishes. His hair was a gold-brown, and it was long, falling in waves almost to his shoulders. He was dressed all in white—shirt, pants, shoes. He had to be at least twenty. And he was absolutely gorgeous.

When she finally found her voice, it quavered. "Who are you?"

"I don't know," he said simply.

Other Avon Books in the
LAST ON EARTH *Trilogy*
by Marilyn Kaye

LAST ON EARTH

BOOK TWO:
THE
CONVERGENCE

MARILYN KAYE

AVON BOOKS NEW YORK

For Isabelle, Christophe and Thomas Clerc,
with love from Tatie

AVON BOOKS, INC.
1350 Avenue of the Americas
New York, New York 10019

Copyright © 1998 by Marilyn Kaye
Excerpt from *Last on Earth, Book Three: The Return* copyright © 1998 by Marilyn Kaye
Published by arrangement with the author
Visit our website at **http://www.AvonBooks.com**
Library of Congress Catalog Card Number: 98-92794
ISBN: 0-380-79833-6

First Avon Books Printing: December 1998

AVON TRADEMARK REG. U.S. PAT. OFF. AND IN OTHER COUNTRIES, MARCA REGISTRADA, HECHO EN U.S.A.

Printed in the U.S.A.

WCD   10 9 8 7 6 5 4 3 2 1

the harlem streets were completely, utterly silent. Even on 125th Street, a major thoroughfare, Kesha could hear her own footsteps. She took her time, absorbing the atmosphere. It had been a while since Kesha had been uptown in the old neighborhood, home. Four weeks, at least. Since the day of the Disappearance.

She was coming up to her old elementary school now, and she paused to peer through the wire fence at the playground. She could almost see herself there at age eight, her hair gathered in a dozen neat braids, each one punctuated with a color ribbon to match whatever sweater she was wearing. Pals from childhood often told her she dressed better then than she did now, at age seventeen. That was because her mother was in charge back then, and she wouldn't let Kesha out of the house until she was fit to be on the cover of *Vogue*, kiddie version. If Mama could see her now, in her beat-up baggy overalls, a jersey with a hole at one elbow, her dark curls pulled back messily with a band, she'd have a fit. But Mama wasn't going to see her now, so she had nothing to worry about.

She moved on, past the coffee shop where

Daddy used to take her and her brothers for hot fudge sundaes on special occasions. She passed Hauser's Shoes, where old Mr. Hauser had fit her for a new pair of patent leather Mary Janes every Easter. She passed the corner where the boys would hang out with their boom boxes, chanting along with their favorite rap songs. Across the street was the church where one of her brothers sang in the choir.

Then she turned onto the street she had called home.

So many people, even some of her friends, had a twisted image of Harlem. They saw it as a land of drug dealers, drive-by shootings, gang wars. They didn't know about streets like this one, lined with leafy trees, where beautifully restored historic homes reflected the pride of their owners. Kesha had lived in one of those houses with her mother and father, her two older brothers, and her grandmother.

She walked up the steps of the stoop where she used to sit on hot summer nights, licking on a Popsicle. With her hand on the doorknob, she hesitated. She took a deep breath, and walked in.

Waves of memory washed over her, and suddenly her eyes were stinging. The scent of the potpourri her grandmother loved was still in the air. She didn't linger to check out anything else that would bring back feelings. Hurrying up the stairs, she went directly to her old bedroom.

From the back of her closet, she dug out an old knapsack, and began to stuff it with the items she'd come here for—books, including her prized Maya Angelou poetry collection, autographed by the poet herself. Some framed family photos. The watch that had been her sixteenth birthday present. A favorite sweatshirt, a couple of flannel nightgowns. Her old broken-in hiking boots.

She didn't really *need* those hiking boots. There were brand new ones in her closet downtown. She had gotten them a few weeks ago at Bloomingdale's, where she and Donna and Martina had gone on a shopping spree. She remembered how strange it had been back then, walking out of a department store with items they hadn't purchased. They'd felt like shoplifters. But there were no salespeople, no one to pay, so they didn't have any choice. Of course, she didn't feel strange about it anymore. No one did. They were accustomed to taking what they wanted, when they wanted it, at whatever store happened to be convenient.

No, she didn't need her old boots. But if anyone asked why she'd gone home, she could say it was because there was nothing like old broken-in boots, and it would be ages before the new ones would be that comfortable. And since she was here, she might as well grab some personal mementos. There were some things a person couldn't find in a department store. But the boots provided her with a good excuse, so no one would suspect she'd gone suddenly sentimental.

Once the knapsack was full, she zipped it up, threw it over her shoulder, and ran downstairs and out the door. Outside, she walked briskly, and tried not to think about the total absence of life around her. Sometimes she felt like she could almost *hear* the silence.

She tried not to look at the houses that stood empty, waiting to be lived in again. There was a motorcycle parked in front of one of them, and she considered taking it back downtown. But it was a cool, autumn day, a nice day for a walk. Besides, she was in no rush to get back there. She would only become more and more frustrated, watching the others do nothing.

And they called themselves rebels—hah! Jake Robbins spent his days in solitary jogging, swimming, working out—and for what? Not in preparation for battle with the Community, that was for sure. Jake wasn't the warrior type. He probably just wanted to look good when and if his girlfriend, ex-supermodel Ashley Silver, ever came back to him. Kesha could tell him not to hold his breath. Ashley would never leave the comfort of private rooms in a nice hotel for a futon on the floor of a health club.

And Kesha's pal, Martina Santiago, who had been full of spirit just a week ago, now spent her time alone, moping, probably in delayed mourning for the loss of her identical twin sister. That was sad, of course, but they'd all lost families and friends. Moping wouldn't bring anyone back.

What kind of rebels spent their days in isolation, not communicating, caught up in their own little worlds? Maybe she wasn't being fair. Some people needed the safety and security of something they could call a home. They were still in a state of shock.

What Kesha wanted to say to all of them was this: Get over it! It was time to shake off the shock and the fear and the sadness and move on. They'd had a month to deal with it, wasn't that enough?

A month . . . now that was hard even for Kesha to grasp. Sometimes it seemed like yesterday.

Other times she felt as if it had been many months, years even, since D-day.

That's what they called it now, D-day, for lack of a better word. Some thought the D stood for death. Kesha's group believed it meant disappearance. One month ago, twenty-five seniors from Madison High School had emerged from an underground classroom to find that every other person on earth had vanished.

Kesha had turned off 125th Street, and now she was heading down Amsterdam Avenue. Her pace slowed as she walked through the campus of Columbia University, with its trees and grass and stately buildings. The silence here seemed more normal. This could be the semester break, when the students were away. Or she could pretend this was exam week, and everyone was in the library studying.

She'd hoped to be a freshman here next fall. Her grades were high, and if she did well enough on her SATs, she'd have a good chance of getting in. Her parents would want her to live at home and commute, but she'd been wondering if it wouldn't be more fun to live in the dorm . . .

She shook her head vigorously, as if the action would knock these foolish thoughts out of her mind. Universities, dorms, SATs . . . these things had no place in their world today.

Or maybe she should say, their two worlds. After D-day, they'd begun their new life together, all twenty-five of them. In a small Soho hotel, they settled down and called themselves the Community. Former senior class president Travis Darrow took over, with their blessing.

Well, most of them gave their blessing. Kesha

didn't think much of Travis. Some people might assume they would have a relationship of some sort, since they were the only African Americans to survive the Disappearance. But that common denominator didn't bring them any closer together. And the fact that Travis had beat her out in the election for senior class president certainly didn't help.

As far as Kesha was concerned, Travis was nothing more than a would-be politician, with all the flaws that role implied. He came from a political family—in fact, his father was one of the most influential African Americans in government. Travis looked good, in a well-groomed preppy way. He spoke well, and he had the kind of confidence that came from growing up surrounded by wealth and important people. Travis was a class act, Kesha had to acknowledge that. She had to admit that he had charisma, and all those years in bureaucratic school politics had left him with some real organizational skills. But in Kesha's opinion, that smooth, confident, in-charge exterior was a facade. Her own observations of Travis had led her to believe that he was actually an insecure mess, and power was the only thing that made him feel good about himself.

Travis had goals. "We are the world," he said. "We're all that's left. We have to get over our grief and accept that. And in the memory of those who are gone, we have to re-create a civilization."

Kesha thought she knew why Travis didn't want them to grieve too much. Grief could lead to anger, which could lead to action. He didn't want any investigation of the situation, any disruption of the status quo. He had a nice little world now, that he could take over and control. If everyone would put their faith in him, he could direct the creation of a new society.

But not everyone could function easily in Travis's rigid society. There were too many rules and regulations, committees, assigned duties and responsibilities, curfews, that sort of thing. And not everyone was so quick to accept that nothing could be done about what had happened.

Kesha and some others who were dissatisfied with the state of things had turned to Jake for help. For the life of her, Kesha couldn't remember *why* they'd chosen Jake. Sure, he was a nice guy. He was good-looking, too, in a low-key way, with strong features and warm brown eyes. He wrote sensitive editorials for the school paper, and he'd written a couple of poems for the school literary magazine. He didn't have what could be called a magnetic personality, he certainly wasn't the life of any party, but he had a deliberate, thoughtful air that inspired trust. He seemed like someone who wouldn't freak out easily.

Jake had led the so-called rebels to a new home, a health club just across the street from the hotel. It was supposed to be a temporary stop, providing them with a moment to catch their collective breath, to give others a chance to join them, and then to take off, in search of—what? Answers. Answers to questions like, why had it happened, who made it happen? Why were twenty-five high school seniors the only people left on earth? Where was everyone else? And would they be back?

But it had been a week now since the rebels had left the community, and they were still living much as they had before, only without the amenities of their former private hotel rooms. Of course, Jake hadn't tried to establish the kind of rules and regulations that Travis had imposed. Jake had done nothing at all. His air of quiet deliberation had given way to something that resembled sleepwalking. Everyone was doing his or her own thing, which was better than following Travis's rules, but it wasn't leading them anywhere.

At 86th Street, Kesha turned east. A few minutes of walking brought her to Central Park, 840 acres of meadows, lakes, fountains and playgrounds. This was where they should all be right now. Not huddled together in a pseudo-society, or living as totally unconnected individuals.

Maybe unconnected wasn't the right word. The rebels spoke to each other. They said ''hi'' and ''Let's get something to eat,'' stuff like that. Sometimes they watched videos together on the large-screen TV in the lounge, and talked about them afterward. But that was about it. They didn't talk about anything meaningful, anything real. They weren't connecting.

At least, most of them weren't connecting. Alex and Shalini, two misfits, had connected in a very weird way. What a pair they made—the quiet, mousy little Indian girl and the angry, sullen boy who looked like he was born in a leather jacket. The least communal of the group, they'd been the first to leave the Community. But they'd returned, with a revelation.

Kesha walked into Central Park on the 86th Street Transverse Road. That led her directly onto the vast expanse of green known as the Great Lawn, where she could look for herself at the phenomenon she'd only seen in the photographs Alex and Shalini had brought back with them.

It was a huge, darkened area of crushed grass, still plainly visible after a month. Something very large and round and heavy had been there, and had left. The photos Kesha had seen were taken from one of the highrise buildings on Fifth Avenue. From those photos, she knew that the area formed a perfect circle, with four evenly spaced darker lines extending from it. Landing gear, someone had suggested.

So now they had a clue; they had evidence. It was possible that everyone on earth hadn't just disappeared, that they hadn't simply vanished into thin air. Maybe they were taken away.

They should all be here right now, all the rebels. They should be combing the grass, climbing the trees, searching for more clues. They could be lighting bonfires, shooting fireworks, anything to draw attention to themselves. They could raid a television station, get their hands on satellite connections, communications equipment. Working together, they could figure out how to operate sophisticated technology. Cameron Daley was a real techie; he could come up with the means to relay messages. And receive them, if anyone else was sending them. Okay, maybe it wouldn't be easy, but they could be trying, they could be doing something.

As Kesha walked around the crushed grass, she looked up into a blue, cloudless sky, and she felt so alone. She knew everyone thought of her as a confident young woman, a big girl with a strong personality—some might call it pushy—and an ambitious nature. But here, in the middle of this mystery, she was small and helpless. There was nothing she could do on her own.

She never thought she'd find herself alone like this. If no one else, her best friend should be here with her. But Donna had turned her back on the rebels to stay behind in the Community. To stay with Travis, in hopes of rekindling a relationship they once had. Donna herself had said it wasn't much of a relationship, it never had been, and Kesha had thought Donna was over it. Sometimes, Kesha felt Donna's betrayal was almost as much of a shock as the Disappearance.

So who was left? She could write off the folks across the street in the hotel, Travis's group; they wouldn't help. They'd given up hope; all they wanted to do was survive, and have someone tell them what to do. Even if they wanted to communicate, Travis wouldn't let them. He'd posted guards who monitored their coming and going— for their own protection, he said. He'd convinced them that the rebels were foolish, misguided, and possibly dangerous, and anxious to lure others into their anarchy. Maybe they *were* anarchists, in a way, Kesha thought. They were just a handful of people, each with his or her own agenda.

Cam Daley was a smart guy, but he was more interested in communicating with his computer than with any human beings. Adam Wise, she barely knew—he seemed okay, not a bad guy, just a blank. Alex and Shalini were only interested in each other. David Chu was gorgeous and worthless, a party animal who stayed with the rebels because Travis's restrictions cramped his style.

Then there was Jake, their so-called leader. Kesha had admired Jake. She thought he had intelligence and a quiet courage, strength with sensitivity, determination tempered by a sense of humor. Who would have thought the departure of a girlfriend would put him in such a funk? Everyone had lost people—family, friends, boyfriends and girlfriends. They were all coping, why couldn't he? Ashley wasn't even one of the missing; she was just across the street with the Community.

That was it, that was all of them. The eight rebels. They'd broken away from the Community because they wouldn't accept that nothing could be done, because they wanted to know what happened to their world, and they wanted to do something about it. But what were they doing? Moping, grieving, playing with computers. Nothing. Absolutely nothing.

She involuntarily shivered. It was colder now, and the knapsack was getting heavy. She turned away from the Great Lawn and started back downtown.

two

donna caparelli took special efforts getting dressed that morning. She didn't put on her usual jeans and sweater. Travis liked girls to look chic, so she wore a dress—nothing fancy, just a crisp, beige linen sheath, short enough to be fashionable but not so short that she looked trashy. It wasn't really her taste, but Travis came from a very proper background, and she wanted to please him.

She kept her makeup conservative, too, and she tied her hair back neatly with a small scarf. Examining herself in the mirror, she decided she could pass for one of those Upper East Side debutante girls, the kind Travis grew up with, girls who went to private schools and spent their summers at country estates in the Hamptons. She certainly looked a lot different than she'd looked when they first went out, over a year ago.

What an odd pair they must have seemed. Preppy, conservative Travis, with his sharply pressed chinos and his polo shirts, came from a prominent political family whose picture had appeared in a *Time* magazine article about rising black politicians. Donna, with her big hair, her two-inch bloodred fingernails, her short tight skirts, came from a working class family on Staten Island. They never brought each other to their respective homes. They hadn't discussed it, but it was silently understood that the Darrow family wouldn't consider Donna to be an appropriate companion for their son. And her own parents would throw a fit if they knew she was dating a black guy.

As it was, she didn't have to worry about sneaking behind her parents' back for long. They only went out for a couple of months. He didn't actually dump her. Travis would never behave crudely like that. He'd been a perfect gentleman, claiming that family pressures and the stress of his position as class president made it impossible for him to give her the kind of attention she deserved. She'd been deeply depressed, but she had to admit he'd been kind of sweet about it all.

Kesha didn't think so. At the time, she had told Donna that Travis was using her, going out with her during his campaign for senior class president to prove he wasn't the snob his classmates thought he was. Donna hadn't wanted to believe this, but it wasn't that difficult for Kesha to convince her. After all, Kesha was her best friend. She only had Donna's best interests at heart, and Donna trusted her completely.

Kesha could convince her of just about anything. They met during their freshman year at Madison, where Donna hadn't known anyone. Madison was a magnet school—the students came from all over New York, and they had to pass a test to get in. Donna had only taken the test to keep a grade school friend from Staten Island company. But Donna got in, the friend didn't, and now she was alone in a strange new high school. She couldn't pass up the opportunity, though—everyone knew Madison was one of the best schools in the city. With a degree from Madison, she might even get a college scholarship.

But in that first month of freshman year, Donna felt terribly out of place with all the bright, ambitious, energetic students. Kesha, in particular, had intimidated her. Kesha was in her sociology class, and she seemed so sure of herself. She was quick to express her opinion and jump into any debate. Donna, on the other hand, was a wimp. When she finally got up the nerve to express herself tentatively in class, some snotty jerk ridiculed her comments. She couldn't recall what the subject had been, but she clearly remembered being on the verge of tears.

Kesha had jumped to her defense, supporting Donna's opinion. And after class, she'd invited Donna to join her and others at lunch. She encouraged Donna to sign up for student activities and sponsored her for a social action committee. Suddenly, Donna had people to hang out with, and she wasn't lonely anymore.

At that point, she would have become Kesha's willing slave. Fortunately, Kesha didn't want a slave, just a really good friend, and Donna was happy to comply. Over the next couple of years, their friendship deepened and intensified until they knew each other so well they could practically read each other's minds. Looking back now, she realized it was funny, in a way, that her best friend and the boy she adored were both black.

But not friends. Kesha had never liked Travis. She'd run against him for class president, and she'd lost. That had to fuel her feelings about him. When he broke up with Donna, that gave Kesha another reason to dislike him.

Donna had never been able to convince Kesha that she was wrong about Travis. She realized now that he must have been just as heartbroken at the time as she was. She would never forget the look on his face, just one week ago, when she told him she had decided to leave the rebels and return with him to the Community. His joy had been unmistakable.

She hadn't looked to see Kesha's reaction to her sudden decision. She didn't need to. She knew her best friend felt betrayed and abandoned.

Even now, a week later, Donna's conscience bothered her. She remembered how, on Disappearance Day, she'd been so relieved to have Kesha there with her. In the midst of the shock and despair, they'd both marveled at the good fortune which had placed them in the same class, the class that survived. She could only hope that someday Kesha would come to understand why Donna had to leave. Their friendship may have been intense, but love was the most powerful emotion of all, strong enough to make a girl run out on her best friend.

And this was love, she assured herself. She knew this was true, despite the fact that Travis had never used that four-letter word. After all, she couldn't feel this committed to someone who didn't love her back.

Finally satisfied with her appearance, she stepped back from the mirror. Her efforts weren't just for Travis; others would be noticing her too. As the girlfriend of the acknowledged leader of the Community, she had a certain image to maintain, a standard to live up to. At least, that's what Travis was always telling her. "You're like a First Lady," he told her. "I want to be proud of you."

That stung a little. If he really loved her, wouldn't he just naturally be proud of her? But then, Travis's notion of love seemed to be different from hers. Donna's notion involved a lot of affection, in words and action. She liked snuggling, and sweet talk, and major body contact. Travis went through the motions, he did what he was supposed to do, but he didn't act like he was really into it. It was like his mind was always somewhere else. And he never said The Words. Whenever Donna whispered, "I love you," he only mumbled something like "Yeah, me too."

Still, in public, he behaved like a boyfriend and he treated her like a girlfriend. He held her hand, he put his arm around her. At meals, he always saved the seat beside him for her. Everyone acknowledged that they were a couple. She had to admit, people were friendlier and a lot more respectful to her now than they'd been back in the old days at Madison High.

She left her room and took the elevator to the top floor, where Travis lived in the penthouse suite. No one objected last week when he'd left his ordinary room at the hotel and moved up there. It would be like objecting to a newly elected U.S. President moving into the White House.

Maura Kelly had expressed surprise, though. "Why doesn't he move out of the hotel to someplace fancier?" she'd asked Donna. "Then you two could live together and have more privacy."

"Because he wants to stay close to the people," Donna told her. "And he doesn't think it would look right if we lived together. He told me he feels like he needs to set a moral example for everyone."

Maura had accepted that explanation. With her eyes shining in admiration, she'd said, "That's so like Travis, to put others before himself." Donna suspected that Maura was a little bit in love with him. But that didn't bother her. Maura was a little bit in love with every guy who walked the face of the earth. Not that there were many of them anymore.

Besides, practically all the girls in the Community were a little bit in love with Travis. That wasn't anything new. Back in the old days, girls flirted with him like mad, and he accepted this easily. Donna didn't mind. At least he never took advantage of their attentions.

The elevator doors opened on the penthouse floor. Two guys jumped from the table where they were playing cards. When they saw her emerge from the elevator, they visibly relaxed.

She smiled brightly at them. "Hi Scott, Kyle. What's new?"

The boys exchanged looks, as if they were passing a signal. Then Scott spoke. "Look, Donna, we were wondering . . ." He hesitated.

"What?" Donna prompted him.

"Could you, maybe, ask Travis if we could set up a TV out here, with Nintendo?"

"Why don't you ask him yourself?" Donna wanted to know.

"Because he'll think we'll start goofing around out here," Kyle told her. "But we'd still do our job. And we'd keep the sound low so we'd hear if anyone approaches. I mean, it's not as if there's a constant stream of enemies pouring in here."

"But we'd be prepared just in case," Scott added hastily.

Donna was getting used to this—people approaching her to ask Travis for favors. These two guys, for example, never spoke to her before D-day. She knew perfectly well that a lot of people were friendly to her only because she was close to their leader. But she didn't care, she enjoyed being important.

She smiled graciously. "I'll see what I can do."

But when she went into Travis's suite, she saw immediately that this wasn't a good time to ask for any favors. He was huddled in the living room with his closest advisors, Mike and Carlos, and he didn't seem particularly thrilled to have his session interrupted.

"It's ten o'clock," Donna said.

He looked at her blankly.

"We're going upstate, remember? To see the foliage."

He frowned for a second, and then his expression morphed into one she'd become unhappily familiar with—apologetic. "I can't, Donna, not today. We're working on the budget."

"I still don't understand why we need a budget," Mike said. "We can just take anything we want."

"It's not civilized to live like that," Travis said. "If we're going to make a real society, we need a monetary system."

He turned to Donna, and he saw the disappointment on her face. "I'm sorry, Donna. We'll go another time."

She didn't want to pout in front of the others, but she was very frustrated. "We've already missed the peak of the season, Travis. The leaves are falling, there won't be much left to see pretty soon.''

Now Travis's voice was becoming testy. ''Donna, I've got more important things to do than look at autumn leaves.''

''How were you going to get upstate?'' Mike asked. ''Bike? The highways are clogged with cars and trucks, you know.''

Carlos agreed. ''I don't think anyone's been more than ten miles outside the city.''

''We were going to fly,'' Donna said wistfully. ''Travis was going to take me up in a plane. It would have been my first time.''

Both Mike and Carlos stared at Travis in astonishment. ''You can fly a plane?'' Carlos asked.

''I took some lessons,'' Travis admitted.

''He's got a real pilot's license,'' Donna said proudly. Travis shot her a warning look. She remembered that he didn't want this fact publicized, for fear people would start begging him to take them places.

''Man, if I had a pilot's license,'' Mike said, ''I'd go all over the world.''

''Have you flown over the area?'' Carlos asked him. ''Have you checked out the region, to see if anyone's out there?''

''There's no point,'' Travis said. ''No one's out there, you know that. Donna, I'll talk to you later.''

She clearly had been dismissed. And it wasn't the first time he'd blown her off like this. Three times this week, they'd had plans to do something special, just the two of them together, and three times he'd canceled. At least she didn't have to worry that he might be seeing another girl. She knew who her rival was—the Community.

Outside the room, she pushed the elevator button.

"Did you ask him?" Scott asked eagerly.

"Huh?" The elevator arrived.

"About getting Nintendo."

"He's busy," Donna told the boys. "This isn't a good time." She stepped into the elevator not lingering for their reaction. On impulse, she pressed the button for the third floor instead of her own. When the elevator stopped, she walked out and went directly to a door.

Knocking lightly, she called out, "Ashley? It's me, Donna."

The girl who opened the door looked sleepy, as if she'd just gotten out of bed. There were deep dark circles under her eyes. The oversized T-shirt she wore swallowed her body, making her appear small and childlike, in spite of her height. The fact that she was completely bald only exaggerated her fragile air.

But even in her shapeless clothes, with her bald head, she was still beautiful. She still looked like the supermodel she'd been back in the old days.

"Hi," she said vaguely. She blinked, as if she was having trouble bringing Donna into focus.

"You okay?" Donna asked.

"Sure." She opened the door wider. "Come on in."

It dawned on Donna that she'd never been in Ashley's room before. It looked like any other room at the hotel, with one difference.

"Good grief," Donna said, moving closer to a framed painting on the wall. "That looks like real art."

"It is," Ashley replied. "It's a Monet. I got it from the Metropolitan Museum of Art."

"You're kidding. You just walked into the museum and took a painting?"

"I was with Jake," Ashley said. "He said it was a shame that all these great works of art were hidden away in the museum."

Donna nodded. "It's not like there are tourists running through the place anymore."

"We decided it would be okay to take some paintings back here. At least that way, they could be appreciated."

"Do you miss Jake?" Donna asked gently. From what she'd observed, Ashley and Jake had been getting into a heavy relationship before the split.

"Sometimes," Ashley admitted. She went to a window and looked out. With her back to Donna, she said, "It wouldn't have worked out. He didn't really love me."

Donna recalled the way Jake used to act around Ashley. "It looked like love to me."

"He loved the way I look," Ashley said simply. "He always talked about how beautiful I am." She touched her head. "He was more upset when I lost my hair than I was."

"But that didn't change his feelings about you," Donna pointed out.

Ashley shrugged. "That didn't matter. He couldn't see past the beauty." She spoke in a matter-of-fact way, and Donna knew she wasn't being conceited, because it was the truth.

Donna had barely known Ashley at all, before. No one had: Ashley lived a different sort of life, a glamorous life, traveling, meeting celebrities, appearing in magazines. She wasn't at school very often, and when she was there, she kept pretty much to herself. Most people thought she was a snob.

She didn't behave snobbishly now, but she was still different. Her racially-mixed background—a black mother and a white father with some Asian blood—accounted for her exotic beauty. Her travels and experiences had given her a sophistication far beyond her years, and certainly beyond that of her classmates. There was still an element of mystery about her.

Maybe that was why Donna had been seeking her out lately. Mysteries could be very interesting. "You want to do something today?" she asked hopefully. "We could go to a museum and steal a few more pictures." She could understand why Ashley had done that, but it still felt a little shocking to say.

"No, not today," Ashley said. "I'm kind of tired. I haven't been sleeping well lately. I keep having these dreams . . ."

"What kind of dreams?"

Ashley turned away from the window and looked at her. "Crazy dreams. Have you ever had a dream that seemed so real that—that you feel like it really happened? And when you're having the dream, you're not even sure you're actually sleeping? And you wake up feeling exhausted?"

Donna was taken aback by the intensity in Ashley's voice. "No," she said uneasily.

"The people I see in the dreams, it's as if they're standing right in front of me. And I can hear them; I can even smell them! Has that ever happened to you?"

Donna shook her head again. She wasn't sure

she wanted to hear any more about Ashley's weird dreams. She didn't want to start having her own nightmares. "Well, I'd better get going if I'm going to, you know, go anywhere."

Ashley nodded, turning back to look out the window, and Donna escaped. The girl was spooky, she decided. She'd heard stories about how Ashley used to go to wild parties, with jet-set types and Eurotrash. Maybe she'd gotten into drugs back then, and now she was having flashbacks.

In any case, Donna wasn't terribly sorry that Ashley couldn't hang out with her that day. She was realizing now that she wasn't in the mood to hang out with anyone. Within the Community, she had an image, and she had to live up to it. Like Travis always reminded her, she had to be always up, always optimistic and enthusiastic. She represented him, and whatever she did, however she acted, reflected on him. It was a heavy responsibility.

She just couldn't pull it off today. Now, if Kesha were around, that would be different. With Kesha she never had to fake being upbeat and cheerful. When she was feeling down, it was okay. Kesha understood.

And she was feeling down now. She'd been on the edge of contracting the blahs for the past few days, and now she definitely had them. She wondered if women like Hillary Clinton or Martha Washington had ever felt like this. It wasn't easy, being the wife or girlfriend of a man who had the weight of the world on his shoulders. She knew she could never be the number one topic on Travis's mind. She'd just have to learn to live with that.

But that didn't make her feel any better today. She was bored, she was restless, and she was feeling more than a little sorry for herself. She had to get out of here.

The buddy at the door that day was James Dupont, not one of Donna's favorite people. He took his job very seriously. And Donna was about to break two rules—she was going out alone, and she didn't even know where she was going. But this was the kind of situation where her role as the Community's version of First Lady came in handy. James wasn't going to give her a hard time.

"I guess Travis knows what you're up to," he said.

"What do you think?" she replied coolly. So she didn't even have to tell a lie.

She understood why Travis had imposed these rules. The safety of the Community was his first priority. No one knew for certain why the rest of the world had disappeared, and the danger could still be lurking out there somewhere. Or someone could get hurt accidentally, or lost. It was safer to travel with a companion.

Travis had another concern now, too. He'd spoken about it just two nights ago, at the weekly Community meeting. "The rebels are quiet now, but that doesn't mean we can rest easy. They could be making plans to increase their power and control. They may attempt to kidnap Community members, and hold them for ransom. Or they may be developing brainwashing techniques, to convince kidnapped members to stay with them. In any case, we must be careful, and not put ourselves in vulnerable positions."

Personally, Donna had thought he sounded a little paranoid, and she wasn't alone. Someone in the group actually laughed. But Travis kept his cool. "Yes, I know that sounds dramatic, but I'd rather err on the side of being too cautious. We can hope for the best, but we must expect the worst."

As the leader's girlfriend, she was a prime target. If Travis found out she was traveling on her own, he'd be very angry at her. But he didn't have to find out. And if he did . . . well, at least she'd get some attention from him.

Now that she was outside, free to take off, she still had no idea what to do or where to go. From where she stood, she could see the health club, right across the street. She wondered if Kesha was in there, right that minute. For one fleeting, wild and crazy moment, she considered going over there and walking in. But of course, she couldn't do that. It would be a betrayal of the Community. Not to mention Travis.

As she stood there, considering her options, two other Community girls came out of the hotel. "Hi, Donna," they chirped in chorus. Donna smiled benevolently and returned the greeting. "What are you guys up to?" she asked.

"We're going to Elizabeth Arden to give each other facials," Courtney replied. "They have this great steaming machine, it gets rid of all your zits. Want to come with us?"

Donna had already given herself two facials that week. She couldn't spend her whole life having beauty treatments. "No, thanks," she said. "I'm going home."

The words slipped out easily, as if she'd known for some time what her plans for the day were.

"Home?" Nicole asked. "You mean, where you lived before?"

Donna nodded. "Staten Island."

The more she thought about it, the better the idea sounded. She hadn't been back there at all since everything happened. Other kids had made trips to their homes, to collect personal items, photographs, that sort of thing. But they were kids with happy memories of home and family. Donna's home had been a raging battlefield between an abusive father and an alcoholic mother. Her older sister had become pregnant in high school, and had been forced to marry her scumbag boyfriend. Donna's father assumed that Donna would follow in her sister's footsteps, and treated her like a slut-in-training. It was not a happy home.

Still, it was a destination. And a search of her room could possibly provide her with an item or two that she wouldn't mind having. Like her old, raggedy teddy bear with its missing ear.

It would be a substantial trip, and it would keep her occupied most of the day. Unless she wanted to try sailing a ferry boat from lower Manhattan, the only way to get there would be through Brooklyn and then across the Verrazano Narrows Bridge. She started down the street, stopping when she spotted a motorcycle that didn't look too complicated.

But her neat, proper dress seemed inappropriate for the ride, and despite the fact that it was highly unlikely she'd run into anyone, she decided to change clothes. She stopped at the first Gap she came to, and emerged moments later in new jeans, a black turtleneck, and sneakers. She considered picking up a leather jacket somewhere, but it was warm for October. At least now she looked like someone who should be on a motorcycle.

She biked across the Brooklyn Bridge, and through the borough that had once had the highest population in New York. It was just as deserted as Manhattan, but the streets weren't quite as cluttered with cars and trucks. She passed through some cute neighborhoods, and wondered if Travis could be persuaded to let the Community roam around more. It was silly to keep them all cooped up in a small Soho hotel when there was this huge city to play in. Sometimes she felt like she was trapped there, and she knew others had to be feeling that way, too.

No, that was disloyal thinking. Travis only wanted to protect them, it wasn't as if he was trying to control them or anything like that.

She traversed the borough, from the dignified brownstones of Brooklyn Heights to the neat small houses in Bay Ridge. Finally, she came to the Verrazano Narrows Bridge. Staten Island was on the other side. There were a lot of cars on the bridge, so she had to slow down and weave in and out and around them.

She paused completely at one point, to estimate whether or not she had the space to squeeze the bike between two huge moving vans. That was when she thought she saw some movement.

She'd never needed glasses, but even so, she blinked a couple of times and rubbed her eyes. It was just a flash of white, almost totally hidden behind a vehicle, but something definitely was moving on the side of the bridge. A dog, maybe? For a while, after the vanishing, wild dogs had roamed the streets of New York. But no, all animals had disappeared, soon after the people.

She braked her bike, and edged closer. It was a person, a boy, standing by the rail, head bowed as if he were looking down at the water. His back was to her, so she couldn't recognize him. How strange that someone else would be out here today, she thought. Her heart skipped a beat. Maybe it was one of the rebels.

So what if it is, she told herself. They're just your former classmates. You don't have to be afraid of them. And what if this person did kidnap her? At least it would relieve her boredom . . .

She moved closer. Then she called out tentatively, "Hello?"

The guy had to have heard her, there wasn't another sound around them. But he didn't turn around. As she watched, he stepped up on a ledge by the rail. Then, to her horror, he pulled himself up to a bar closer to the top of the rail. She realized what he was about to do.

"No!" she cried out. She dashed toward him. He didn't move. So she did the only thing she could think of—she grabbed his leg and pulled. She must have taken him by surprise, because despite the fact that he was taller and bigger than she was, he fell back onto the bridge.

Face to face, she saw immediately that he wasn't one of the rebels. He wasn't a member of the Community, either. He was no one she'd ever seen before in her life.

He gazed at her vaguely, with the lightest, bluest eyes she'd ever seen. His face was handsome, in a movie-star way—square jaw, straight nose, no blemishes. His hair was a gold-brown, and it was long, falling in waves almost to his shoulders. He was dressed all in white—shirt, pants, shoes. He wasn't a boy either—she could see that now. He had to be at least twenty. And he was absolutely gorgeous.

When she finally found her voice, she scolded him fervently. "You shouldn't even think about that! Life will get better!"

He looked at her blankly. Suddenly, she wasn't so sure of herself.

"Weren't you about to jump into the river?"

"No."

"What were you doing?"

"Looking at the water."

She shouldn't have jumped to conclusions. This guy didn't look suicidal. "Who are you?"

His eyes became more focused, and they hit her like a blue laser. "I don't know," he said simply.

"You don't know?" she repeated. "You don't know who you are? You don't know your name?"

"My name is Jonah."

"What are you doing here, Jonah?"

"I don't know."

"Where do you come from? How did you get onto this bridge?"

"I don't know," he said again.

"You mean, you don't remember anything?" She made a vague gesture. "You don't know what happened?"

"I remember nothing," he said.

Donna drew in her breath sharply. She had a memory from a soap opera she used to watch religiously. A character showed up one day in the hospital, and he didn't know who he was or what he was doing there. The doctors said he had amnesia.

"How frightening," she whispered.

"Yes," he said.

To hear words like that coming from such a strong-looking, handsome man made her insides go weak. She took his hand.

"Don't be afraid," she said. "I'll take care of you."

three

walking the 80 plus blocks from Central Park to Greenwich Village was good for Kesha. The brisk trek energized her. But a cloud of gloom descended on her as she crossed Houston Street. This wide street represented the boundary between the area of New York known as Greenwich Village and the section called Soho, which stood for South of Houston. It was ironic, in a way. Kesha used to think of Soho as the coolest neighborhood in all of New York. There were hangouts and dance clubs that you couldn't get into unless you were accompanied by a rock star or a supermodel. Through large picture windows, you could see the beautiful people eating in the trendiest restaurants. There was great window shopping, too, with boutiques displaying the hippest clothes around.

Not that Kesha had the money to hang out in Soho. But sometimes, after school, she and Donna would wander down there, to gape at the lifestyle and try to spot celebrities. Then they would move east, to Broadway, and down toward Canal, where they might find cheap imitations of the fashions they'd just seen, sold from racks on the street. Or they'd prowl through vintage clothing shops for something outrageous, like a feather boa or a beaded sweater from the 1950s. Then they'd pig out on cannoli and cappucinos at an Italian coffee shop. They had a lot of fun back then.

She didn't know what was depressing her more, thinking about those good times with her former best friend, or entering the area which had come to represent a prison for her. She supposed she could just keep on walking, past the health club, beyond Soho, maybe all the way to Battery Park. She could get on a ferry there, figure out how to make it go, and take off to . . . to the Statue of Liberty! She'd always wanted to climb to the top of it. Or she could keep going, past Liberty Island, to . . . to . . . to whatever land mass she reached.

No, she was just putting off the inevitable. She knew she'd end up going back to the health club. She wanted adventure, she wanted to escape, but she didn't want to roam the world all by herself.

What she had to do was use her powers of persuasion to get the others to take off with her, to follow her out of this dismal place. But could her persuasive skills ever be powerful enough to accomplish this? She always thought of herself as a leader in spirit, but she knew she lacked the people skills that could get others to follow her. She didn't have the patience to cajole them. Donna often told her that her aggressive nature turned some people off, and that was why she'd lost the student government election to Travis.

Kesha had trusted Donna's opinion back then, despite the fact that Donna was involved with Kesha's rival. Kesha had considered Donna's relationship with Travis to be a fling, and thought that the friendship between the girls would transcend the couple's romance. How wrong she was.

In any case, she certainly wasn't the leader of the rebels. She found their leader on the balcony track that encircled the health club's swimming pool. Jake spent a lot of time jogging around the track. Kesha wished he would find a more productive way to channel his energies.

He saw Kesha and his pace slowed, but he was still breathing pretty hard when he reached her.

"Hi," he said. "How're ya doing?"

She didn't waste time with greetings. "I have to talk to you," she said. She could hear how harsh that sounded, so she amended the statement to sound less abrasive. "We need to talk."

"Sure," he said. "Want to go down to the snack bar?"

At that moment, the full impact of Jake's physical exertions hit her. She wrinkled her nose and stepped back. "Maybe you want to have a shower first."

"Yeah, okay. I'll meet you down there in half an hour."

She suspected that it wasn't just the recent jog that was producing Jake's pungent odor. The guy looked like he hadn't cleaned himself up in a while. Until recently, Jake had been well-groomed—not particularly fashionable, but neat and clean, in a khaki pants and white shirt way. His bust-up with Ashley had really hit him hard. Amazing, what love—or the loss of love—could do to a person, she thought. Jake had definitely let himself go in the past week.

Now if Alex Popov had started showing signs of deterioration, she wouldn't be so surprised. He'd always looked pretty rough with his scraggly, unkempt hair, and he was perpetually in need of a shave. But when Kesha saw him in the snack bar, she thought he was looking pretty good. He still had that hoodlum style, but he wasn't as grubby as he used to be. She figured that must be Shalini's influence.

He was sitting with Shalini now, in a corner booth. The way Alex grimaced when Kesha walked in, she figured they must have been having some sort of intimate conversation.

"Hi, guys," she said.

Alex didn't respond. Shalini's "hello" was so soft, it was impossible to tell if there was any hostility in her tone. Both of them watched her warily as she went behind the bar and opened the refrigerator. She took out a soda, unscrewed the top, and had almost brought it to her lips when she realized they were still staring at her.

"Am I interrupting something?"

"No," Shalini whispered, but Alex rose.

"C'mon, let's get out of here," he muttered.

"Alex," Shalini said reprovingly, but she got up. She gave Kesha a helpless, apologetic smile and scurried out after him.

Once again, Kesha marveled at what a weird couple they were. They were totally into each other, but there didn't seem to be anything remotely romantic between them. Kesha had had hopes for Shalini when she and Alex returned from their adventure in Central Park. Shalini had been the one who'd convinced Alex to tell the others about their discovery—the circle of flattened grass. She was speaking for herself that day, and she seemed to have convictions. But in the past week, she'd retreated back to being just a shadow of Alex.

With the soda in her hand, Kesha wandered back out into the reception area. She considered rounding up some of the other rebels to join her in meeting with Jake, but decided against it. She didn't want Jake to feel like they were ganging up on him, or attempting an overthrow. Besides, there didn't seem to be anyone around.

No, someone was around. She heard a sound, like a chair scraping against the floor, coming from the office just off the reception area. She rapped on the door. There was no response, but a light push swung it open.

Cam was in there, alone. He was staring at a computer screen.

"Hi, Cam." He didn't move. She spoke louder. "Cam?"

He looked at her through thick wire-rimmed glasses. "Huh?"

"I said 'hi.' "

"Oh. Hi." His eyes returned to the screen. He wasn't being unfriendly, he was just preoccupied with whatever he was doing, which wasn't unusual for Cam. He wasn't exactly Mister Sociable. Cam was the type who'd always preferred books or computers to people.

"What are you doing?" she asked.

He didn't answer immediately. He hit a couple of keys, and then he said, "Look at this."

Kesha came around the desk and peered over his shoulder at the screen. "What am I supposed to be looking at?"

"This." He tapped the screen.

She examined the combination of letters and symbols. They made no sense at all. "It's gibberish," she said.

"That's what it looks like," Cam told her. "But what do you think it is, really?"

She looked again. "Gibberish."

He shook his head. "It's e-mail."

"Huh?"

"I've been sending out e-mail messages all week."

"Who are you sending them to?"

"Addresses that I make up with a random selection of letters and numbers. If the address doesn't exist, the message comes back to me with an 'unknown address' notation. Most of the messages come back that way. But sometimes they don't come back."

Kesha shrugged. "So you accidentally send it to a real address and the messages get through, so what? Nobody's at the other end to receive them."

"That's what I thought, too," Cam said. "But today, I got this." He tapped the screen.

"Oh, Cam, that's not a response to your e-mail."

"No? What would you call it?"

"It's nothing. Nobody wrote that."

"Then how did it get into my inbox?"

Kesha hesitated. "It's—it's electronic garbage. Yeah, that's what it is. Whatever happened on earth a month ago messed up the atmosphere big time, right? The air is probably filled with charged ions and particles, stuff like that." She had no idea what a charged ion or a particle was, but that sounded good. "There must be garbage like that showing up everywhere, like, like static on the radios, or weird color patterns on TV."

"E-mail is transmitted through wires," Cam said. "It's not broadcast."

"Well, whatever," Kesha said. "The atmosphere affected the wires. In any case, it doesn't mean anything."

"Everything means something," Cam said mildly. "How can you know for sure that somebody out there—or something—isn't receiving my e-mail and trying to answer me?"

Kesha tried a different tactic. "Okay, let's say there's something out there. That's why we should be out there too, looking for clues, trying to make contact. We need to communicate, Cam, not sit all day in front of a computer."

"It's the electronic age, Kesha," Cam reminded her. "This is how people communicate."

Kesha took another look at the computer screen. "But this isn't communication, Cam. Like I said, it's gibberish."

"It looks like gibberish," Cam agreed. "Maybe that's because we don't know how to interpret it."

"What are you saying—this is a foreign language?"

"Possibly. Or it could be some sort of code."

Kesha groaned. "And you're just going to sit here for the rest of your life and try to decipher the code."

Cam grinned. "I don't have anything better to do."

Kesha threw up her hands in defeat and walked out.

Jake was already sitting in the snack bar. He didn't seem irritated that Kesha had kept him waiting. He was just staring into space with the glazed expression that had become annoyingly familiar.

"Hi," Kesha said. "Want a soda?"

"No, thanks."

She decided to get right to the point. "Jake, why are we hanging around here?"

Jake looked at her uneasily. "What do you mean?"

He had to know perfectly well what she meant, but she explained anyway. "We broke away from the Community because we didn't like the way Travis was running it, right?"

"Right," Jake said cautiously.

"And it wasn't just because of his rules, it was his attitude. Travis said everything we knew was finished, that we had to accept that fact that we were the only people on earth, and start building a new civilization. Right?"

"Right."

"But we said we wanted to dig deeper into this, and find out what really happened. Explore possibilities, look for answers. Look for *people*, Jake. Don't you remember? Instead of accepting the situation, we were going to change it!"

This time Jake didn't respond. Kesha pressed on.

"But we're not digging deeper, Jake. We're not looking, we're not exploring, we're not doing anything, we're still the last people alive, as far as we know. If we're not going to look for others, why did we bother leaving the Community?"

"You want to go back there?" Jake asked. "You're free to leave whenever you want."

Kesha bit back the urge to scream. "I don't want to go back to the Community, Jake. I want to go forward, I want to move on. We all do, that's why we left! You're supposed to be our leader. Why aren't you leading us?"

Jake shifted uncomfortably in his seat. "I don't think we're ready to take off. Look, Kesha, it's not every day that people walk out of school and find out that the rest of the world has disappeared. That's pretty traumatic, y'know? People need a chance to recover, to recuperate from the shock."

"It's been a month, Jake. We're not that shook up anymore. What we need now is a sense of purpose. We need direction." She leaned across the table. "We need a leader, Jake."

He wouldn't even meet her eyes. Kesha tried to speak gently.

"It's Ashley, isn't it? That's why you won't leave. You want to stay close to her."

Jake looked up. Relief washed over his face. For a second, Kesha thought she might have reached him. Then she realized he was looking beyond her.

"Hey, Adam, what's up?"

Kesha turned to see Adam Wise standing in the doorway. "Not much," he said easily. "I'm doing a food run. You want anything?"

"I'll go with you," Jake said, jumping up. "See ya, Kesha."

He made his escape, and Kesha sank back in her seat. She wasn't ready to admit full defeat yet, though. Maybe she was wrong not to round up some supporters for the confrontation. Well, she'd just have to gather some backup forces and organize another confrontation.

But there weren't many forces left to choose from. Cam was obviously not interested. Shalini and Alex—forget them. Adam—who knew what Adam was thinking? She left the snack bar in search of Martina.

There were no bedrooms in the health club, of course. But the club was big enough so that they'd all been able to carve out personal spaces. Martina had taken over a small room on the second floor where yoga classes had been held.

Martina was reading when Kesha entered. New Age music played softly in the background. Unlike most of the other rooms, this one didn't have a sparse black and white minimalist feeling. The walls were a soft golden color and there were small patterned rugs on the floor. The lighting was dim, and the smell of musk filled the room.

"Are you burning incense?" Kesha asked.

Martina looked up from her book. "Mm. I found it in the storage closet."

"What are you reading?"

"I found this in the closet too. It's called *Tapping into the Unconscious*."

"What is it, a horror story?"

"No, it's nonfiction," Martina told her. "It's about using powers you don't know you have. To . . . to connect with the world that exists beyond the physical world. To reach another plane of understanding, you know."

Kesha didn't know. "Sounds spooky."

"Not really. It makes you think. I mean, maybe things aren't the way we believe they are. Do you ever think about this?"

"No," Kesha said. "I have other things to think about."

"Like what?"

"Martina, we have to do something." She described her unsuccessful meeting with Jake. "I don't want to be talking behind his back. But we're stagnating here. We have to move on, we need to be out there."

"Out where?"

"I don't know! Cental Park, for starters. That's

where something happened. Maybe that's where we could begin trying to make some connections.''

''We could make connections right here,'' Martina murmured.

Kesha frowned. ''What?''

Martina gazed up at her. Her eyes were dreamy. ''Kesha . . . remember when you asked me if there was some sort of special communication between identical twins? And I told you that Rosa and I sometimes felt each other's pain? We knew when one of us was hurt or in trouble.''

''Yeah.''

''I still *feel* it, Kesha. That bond, the special connection, whatever it is, it's still there. If I could concentrate . . . well, I think I can make contact with her.''

''Don't you think it would be easier to make contact if you were outside?'' Kesha asked her.

''Walls don't block communication, Kesha. Feelings do.''

''Huh?''

''It's a spiritual thing, not a physical thing.'' She got up and started toward the closet. ''I know it sounds spacy, but I've been doing a lot of reading about this, and it makes sense. I could give you a book . . .''

''I don't have time to read,'' Kesha said through clenched teeth. ''I'll see you later.''

She wasn't writing off Martina—this other-worldly mood she was in could be just a passing phase. But who was left for her to talk with now? She was feeling very much alone.

She was distracted by a sudden shout, a cry of anger. It seemed to be coming from above her. She ran upstairs and followed the sounds into the room where weight-lifting equipment was stored.

David Chu was on the floor, rubbing his jaw. Alex stood over him, a small barbell held threateningly in his hand.

"What's going on?" Kesha asked in alarm.

Alex was looking ferocious. "You keep your hands off her, Chu, or I'll bash your head in."

"Alex, he didn't touch me," Shalini said in her teeny-tiny voice.

"I just asked her if she wanted to party," David complained. "It's not like I jumped her bones."

Shalini tugged on Alex's arm. "Come on, Alex, let's go."

Alex shot David one last look of pure wrath before allowing himself to be dragged out of the weight room.

"David, what's the matter with you?" Kesha said. "You know better than to mess around with her. I know it's hard for you to believe that a girl exists who can resist you, but you'd better face it."

He got up from the floor and gave her a rueful smile. Objectively, Kesha had to admit that David was an exceptionally good-looking guy, and he did know how to turn on the charm to his advantage. Unfortunately, he was very much aware of this.

But he wasn't going to be able to exert those charms here, and he must have realized this after a week with the rebels. A sweet, innocent girl like Shalini would be scared to death of him. Martina despised David—he used to go with her sister Rosa, and he broke her heart. As for Kesha . . .

"Come on, babe," David said. He slung an arm carelessly around her shoulder. "This place is deadly. Let's get out of here."

Kesha shrugged his arm off. "No thanks, David."

There were some things worse than being totally alone.

From the journal of Jake Robbins:

Ran almost five miles today. I could have gone longer, but kesha interrupted me. She started nagging me again, about getting out of here and moving up to Central Park. And I keep saying we're not ready to leave yet. But I can tell from the way she looks at me, she's not buying that. I can't blame her. It's a pretty lame excuse.

I feel lousy about this. I'm supposed to be the leader here. I should be making some plans, getting us organized. But I've just been so low, I can't get it together. If Ashley was here, it would be different.

Kesha said I didn't want to leave because of Ashley. She's right. At least while I'm here, I can keep an eye on her. Sometimes, I sit at a window and wait, just hoping she'll walk in or out of the hotel so I can catch a glimpse of her.

I know I'm being stupid. And it's not fair to everyone else. But as long as I think there's a chance she might come back, I don't want to leave.

I miss her so much.

four

ashley moved slowly through a field of daisies. She wasn't sure if she was walking, or if she was swimming in an ocean of white and yellow. Her body was weightless, without substance. She was made of air, she was gossamer, her feet didn't even touch the ground as she sailed through the flowers.

She knew he was out there somewhere. He was calling to her, not with words, with something she heard not with her ears, but with her heart and soul. She had to reach him. She didn't know why, but he would tell her. He would show her the way, he would give her the answers.

And she could see him now, a solitary figure, surrounded by a golden light. He was waiting for her, he was reaching out toward her, she was getting closer and closer and closer . . . then he dissolved, the daisies dissolved, and she saw only beige. The beige ceiling in her room.

Much as Ashley wanted to roll over and close her eyes, she knew better. She'd been sleeping a lot lately, too much. Taking naps in the middle of the afternoon—she never used to need that. It wasn't as if she was doing so much during the day that she needed extra sleep. Back in the old days, she could go forever without much sleep.

The old days . . . they seemed so long ago and far away. Another world, another life. It was hard to believe those days had ended just one month ago. It was even harder to believe that they had begun less than three years ago.

Before that, she'd been an ordinary child from an ordinary family in an ordinary home. The only thing that wasn't ordinary about her was her appearance.

She was a walking melting pot of ethnicity. Her father was the offspring of a German Jewish man and a Chinese woman. Her mother was black, with some Native American ancestry. As a child, she was mocked by other children who couldn't figure out what she was. As she grew, she became accustomed to hearing people remark on her creamy café au lait complexion, the cloud of golden curls that looked more like a halo than hair, the slight tilt to her dark brown eyes, her impossibly high cheekbones. She was unusually tall, she was scrawny, and she didn't look like anyone else.

So maybe it wasn't all that remarkable when she was spotted on a plane flight by a modeling agent and signed practically on the spot. At the age of fourteen, practically overnight, childhood ended and she became a full-fledged, beautiful young woman, with money and glamour and a lifestyle that no ordinary teenager would recognize.

She conjured up one day in particular, a couple of years ago . . .

She and her mother had flown all night, from New York to Paris, for her first big runway show with a major French designer. She was so excited, she hadn't slept at all on the plane. When they arrived, a limousine took them directly to their hotel, where she barely had enough time for a shower before she was whisked off for hair styling and makeup. Moments later, she was sauntering down the catwalk, confronting a sea of faces and flashing lights. Step, step, pause, turn, pause, half turn, strike a pose . . . then backstage for a fast change of clothes, then onto the runway again. She did this four times.

It was chaos and celebration backstage, and a glass of something gold and bubbly was thrust into her hand. By the time she realized it wasn't ginger ale, she was already dizzily giddy. Later there were parties, dancing, a midnight ride in a boat on the Seine River . . . did she sleep at all that night?

The next day, she did another show, and the day after that there was a magazine shoot in Rome. More parties, more dancing, more champagne. She was the baby among the beautiful women, the handsome men, but it didn't seem to matter, and she danced till dawn. No, she didn't get much sleep in those days. She didn't need it.

But now she slept a lot. That had to be why she kept having the same dream, over and over again. Actually, the dreams weren't completely identical. In one dream, it was winter, and she was running on snow through silver birch trees. In another dream, it was summer, and she ran along a sandy beach. Sometimes she could feel her hair, the golden curls she'd once had, streaming behind her. But always, in every dream, she was running toward the same figure of a man, a man who was waiting for her. She never reached him. She didn't know why she was trying to reach him. What was even weirder was the fact that she didn't even know who he was.

For a while, she thought it might be Jake. Despite all the problems they'd had during the short time they were a couple, she still had feelings for him. He was her first real romance, and for a while, she had thought it might be love. That notion was still in the back of her mind.

But this wasn't a romantic dream. She didn't feel like she was running to a lover. It was something else.

Her thoughts were interrupted by a sharp knock. "Come in."

The door opened, and Maura Kelly appeared. "You doing anything?" she asked Ashley.

"No."

"Want to go do makeovers?" she asked hopefully. "We haven't tried that Swedish cosmetic place on Greene Street."

This was all Maura ever wanted to do. Ashley didn't think a color existed that hadn't been smeared on their eyelids. "Not really."

Maura's face fell, and Ashley felt a mild pang of guilt. She knew Maura idolized her, and would do anything to hang out with her. In Maura's head, Ashley's life had been a fantasy, a carnival of fame and celebrities, where she was fawned over and catered to. She loved hearing Ashley's stories. It was as if the glitter could somehow rub off on her—no matter how often Ashley reminded her that there was no more glitter. Maybe there never had been glitter.

"We could do something else," Ashley offered. If she wanted to get out of the hotel, she needed Maura, or somebody, to go with her. It was a Community rule. No one was allowed out alone, without a companion. Travis said this was for their own safety.

"Like what?"

Suddenly, Ashley knew what she wanted to do. "Let's go to the library."

"The library?" Maura asked, as if Ashley had just used a foreign word.

"Yeah, the big one on Fifth Avenue. I've gone past it a million times but I've never been inside."

Maura still looked confused. "Why do you want to go inside now?"

"There's something I want to look up."

The prospect clearly didn't thrill Maura, but she was willing to go anywhere if she could go with Ashley. So they checked out with the guard at the door, and headed uptown. Along the way, Ashley entertained her with the story of one of her so-called adventures.

"You remember that band, Proxy?"

"Of course," Maura said, "they were huge! Did you meet them?"

"Yeah, I was invited backstage after one of their concerts. I met the lead singer."

"Ooh," Maura squealed. "He was gorgeous! What was he like?"

He was boring, Ashley remembered. Boring, and not very bright. He wasn't even much of a singer. But that wasn't what Maura wanted to hear. "Nice," she said. "Sexy."

For the remainder of the walk, Maura asked non-stop questions about the lead singer, while Ashley struggled to remember enough to provide answers. When she couldn't remember anything, she made stuff up. What did it matter? It wasn't like this information was going to appear in a tabloid tomorrow.

Finally, they reached the huge building, with the two stone lions watching over the entrance, like proud guardians of the knowledge within. Walking toward the door, Ashley couldn't help thinking that this was a memorial to a civilization that would never exist again. Inside, the dignity of the library was awesome. Ashley just stood there for a moment, trying to absorb the intellectual power, the magnitude, of this great monument to knowledge.

Maura was less enthusiastic in her response. "This place is creepy," she declared. "What are you looking for exactly?"

"I want to learn about dreams. How to interpret them."

"Oh. What kind of dream?"

She wasn't about to tell Maura the whole story. "Just dreams in general."

It had been a while since she'd been in a library, and she learned that times had changed. There were no card catalogs anymore. You had to search for books on a computer, which, fortunately, was still operational. Even more fortunately, the computer was "user-friendly," and Ashley was able to identify some call numbers. Armed with these numbers, she went into the stacks and found the books. She brought a pile of them out into the massive reading room, where she placed them on one of the handsome dark wood tables and sat down to read.

Maura also opened a book, and flipped through some pages. "Listen to this." She read aloud. " 'A common dream image has to do with losing teeth. There are many reports of dreams in which people open their mouth and their teeth fall out. Popularly interpreted as a pemonition of death, this loss of teeth actually signifies the subject's belief that he is not being heard.' ''

"That's interesting," Ashley said. But no teeth had fallen out in her dreams lately. She plunged into the index of the first book. But she wasn't even sure what she should be looking for in terms of symbols. Flowers, trees, sand? No, those weren't the important elements. Running, maybe. Or the image of a man.

Maura soon became bored with the books, and went off in search of something to amuse herself with. Ashley continued to pore over the index, looking for words that related in some way to her dream. Then she would turn to the page where she could learn something about the word.

She couldn't find much, and it wasn't the easiest material to read. A lot of the writing consisted of heavy, psychological-sounding descriptions that she could barely understand. She couldn't find anything that related to her dream.

"When a woman dreams of a man," she read, "he represents the strong, assertive side of the woman. The other person in a dream mirrors the dreamer." That wasn't much help. Under "running," she found references to escape, danger, and fear. That didn't tell her anything either.

Maura returned. "Look what I found!" It was a fashion magazine, and Maura had opened it to a page on which Ashley saw a picture of herself. "That's you! And that dress is gorgeous! Do they ever let you keep the clothes you model?"

Ashley studied the picture. The sleek, rose-colored off-the-shoulder dress meant nothing to her—she had no memory of it. But the street scene in the background brought the actual shoot back into her mind. "Corey took those pictures in Milan."

"Who's Corey?"

"A photographer. He was so good. I remember how happy I'd be when I'd show up for an assignment and find out that he was going to be taking the pictures."

Maura shivered in delight. "I saw a show about fashion photographers on MTV once. They're pretty wild, aren't they?" She pretended to hold a camera in front of her eyes. " 'Beautiful, baby, I love it, I love it, fabulous, darling, give it to me, more like that, yes, yes . . .' "

Ashley had to laugh at Maura's fairly accurate imitation of a typical fashion photographer. But Corey hadn't been like that. "He was different."

"How?"

"Just . . . different."

Maura wagged her eyebrows. "Oh, I get it. Were you guys, you know, together?"

"Oh no, nothing like that," Ashley said. "But he was a friend, a truly nice person. He wasn't shallow, like a lot of those people. He didn't care about being famous, he wasn't into the fashion scene. He thought of his photography as art, not just a way to sell clothes."

"Oh." Maura had lost interest in Corey. "Listen, do we have to stay here much longer?"

Ashley closed her book. This wasn't getting her anywhere, and she owed Maura a little fun. "No. Let's go check out the shoes at Saks."

Later on the way back to the hotel, swinging a bag that contained half a dozen pairs of shoes,

Maura's face took on an unusually pensive expression. "You know what's sad?"

Ashley could think of a million sad things. "What?"

"Like, right now, we can pick up the best fall fashions. We can have anything we want, everything that was shown in the magazines, and it's all free. But in the spring, there won't be any new spring clothes. What are we going to wear?"

Ashley had to smile. Sometimes, she thought it would be nice to be as shallow as Maura. Maura probably never had weird dreams.

They had turned onto their street now, and Ashley squinted. "Who's that with Donna?"

"It looks like a man," Maura said. "It *is* a man." She gasped. "And I've never seen him before!"

Neither had Ashley. Their steps quickened as they hurried to catch up with Donna and the stranger. When they reached them, they could see that Donna was bursting with news.

"This is Jonah," she proclaimed. "Jonah, this is Ashley and Maura."

The man had the bluest eyes Ashley had ever seen, the kind she thought you could only have with colored contact lenses. His hair was unfashionably long, like a hippie from the sixties, and a little scraggly, but he was still remarkably handsome, with delicate features and smooth skin.

"Hello," he said.

Maura was gaping. "Where did you come from?"

"I don't know," he replied.

"He has amnesia," Donna declared excitedly. "I found him on the Verrazano Bridge. He doesn't know who he is or how he got there!''

"How do you know your name is Jonah?'' Ashley asked him.

"I don't know,'' he said. "It was just there, in my head.''

"It's called selective amnesia,'' Donna said. "You remember a few little things, like your first name, or your favorite pizza toppings, but nothing else.''

"How do you know so much about it?'' Ashley asked.

"I saw it on a soap opera.''

Maura's eyebrows shot up. "Oh, yeah, I saw that one! The cute guy, the doctor, he was in a head-on collision.'' She turned to the stranger. "Were you in a car accident?''

"I don't know,'' he said again.

Ashley studied him in wonderment. "You mean, you've been wandering around by yourself ever since it happened?''

"Ever since what happened?''

Maura gasped. "You don't know what happened?''

"Maura, shut up,'' Donna chided. "Don't scare him. I'm taking him to see Travis now.'' With a hand on his arm, she led him into the hotel.

In Ashley's eyes, the man didn't look scared, just bewildered, like a lost child. No, not a child. Like a foreigner who didn't speak the language. Donna was probably right, though. They had to break it to him gently.

"Wow,'' Maura breathed. "He must have been hit on the head or something. I wonder how long he's been wandering around?''

"He looks pretty clean and neat for someone

who's been lost for a month," Ashley commented.

"But maybe he wasn't lost for a month," Maura said, her voice rising. "He could have come from another community! Ashley, there could be more people somewhere around here!"

"Oh, Maura," Ashley said. "Don't you think that if there were any other people around, we would have run into them by now?"

"Not necessarily," Maura said. "He could have walked all the way from, I don't know, Alabama or someplace like that."

"No way, you saw him, he hasn't been walking a thousand miles. He doesn't even look tired."

Maura persisted. "Then maybe he just came from Long Island. It's not as if we've sent search parties, checking every town out there. He could be from, from Massapequa. Or Garden Hills."

Ashley didn't bother to point out that any people left in the small cities and towns on Long Island would surely have made their way to Manhattan long ago. She didn't want to throw a wet blanket over Maura's optimism—even if it was totally unrealistic. So she let Maura go on, fantasizing happily about the possibility of more life on earth as she followed Ashley to her room.

There, sitting on Ashley's bed, she continued to chatter as she took her shoes out of the bag and admired them. Holding the brown suede lace-up boots, she said, "Do you think these will go with my camel hair coat?"

"Absolutely," Ashley assured her.

Maura then produced spike-heeled strappy sandles studded with rhinestones. "What do you think of these?"

"Great dancing shoes," Ashley said.

Maura nodded. But as Ashley watched her, the spark of optimism began to fade from Maura's eyes, and she spoke mournfully. "Where am I going to wear them? It's not like there's any place to go dancing." She fell back on Ashley's bed. "You're so lucky, Ashley."

"How's that?"

"Well, at least you had it all for a while. Discos and parties, real night life. Cool places to go, reasons to dress up. I never had any of that. And now it's all gone and I never will."

"It wasn't that great, Maura," Ashley told her. "There were a lot of phonies and creeps around. There were plenty of bad times."

"You haven't told me about any bad times."

Ashley smiled. "Well, they don't make the best stories."

"Tell me about one of the bad times now," Maura urged. "Maybe it will cheer me up."

Ashley thought for a moment. "Okay, remember when I told you about meeting that band, Proxy? Well, I went to this big party for the band after the concert. I was with a couple of other models who were a lot older than me, and they were pretty wild. There were a lot of drugs floating around, really bad stuff. Practically everyone was passing the junk around. I tried to stay away from it all, and I suppose I could have left the party, but I was just getting started in the business and I didn't want the other models to think I was a wuss."

"Did you take drugs?"

"I didn't mean to. But someone spiked my drink with something, I think maybe it was Ecstasy. All I know is that the next thing I remember, I was dancing on a table and taking my clothes off. And some very icky guys were placing bets on who was going to make it with me first.''

Maura was sitting up now, with her mouth open and her eyes the size of saucers. ''Wow, this is like something you read about in the *National Enquirer*,'' she said. ''What happened next?''

''Remember that photographer I told you about, Corey? He was there.'' Ashley tried to think. Her memories of that awful night were cloudy, and what she could remember she had essentially blocked. Bringing it to the front of her mind wasn't very pleasant, but she felt like she owed Maura an idea of what the high life had really been like.

''He rescued me,'' she said simply. ''He pushed one guy off me, and he kicked another one. Luckily, the jerk was too stoned to fight back. Corey threatened to call the police, too. He got me out of there. I could have been raped, or I could have overdosed on something. He saved my life.''

''That was nice of him,'' Maura said.

''More than nice,'' Ashley told her. ''There were some big shots at that party, major industry names. They were pretty pissed off at Corey. They said they were going to have him blackballed, that he'd never get any work again. He risked his whole career to save me.''

She remembered waking up the next morning, fully clothed and untouched, on Corey's sofa. How humilated she'd been, how afraid that her mother or her agent would find out what happened. But Corey had been great. He'd kept everything quiet, and from then on, he'd been her guardian angel. He made it his personal mission to watch out for her at shoots and parties. He filled her in on who to stay away from; he taught her about the pitfalls and dangers of the business. He kept the sleazebags away. He was like a big brother to her, and she could count on him. Corey was a special friend.

Suddenly, she drew her breath in sharply.

"What's the matter?" Maura asked.

"Oh! Nothing, I, uh, just remembered something I have to do."

Maura got up. "Well, I'm going to see if I can find out anything more about this Jonah person. I'll see you at dinner."

"Right," Ashley said faintly. She waited until Maura had left, and then she sank down on her bed and tried to think through the realization that had just hit her.

She knew who the man in her dream was. It was Corey. And not just a memory of Corey—it really was Corey. He existed, he was flesh and blood. Alive.

And he was still trying to save her.

donna felt sorry for Jonah, and she was more than a little embarrassed by her fellow Community members. She had wanted to get him upstairs, sneak him into a room, so he could have a shower and a nap and something to eat before he was presented to Travis. But there were half a dozen kids hanging out in the hotel lobby, and they were spotted before she could get him into an elevator. She was forced to introduce him right then and there, and the next thing she knew, Jonah was being led to an armchair.

They gathered around the stranger, and they were looking at him with frank and unabashed curiosity, like he was some sort of freak. She understood how they felt—after all, it had been a month since any of them had seen a new person, and they'd all been assuming there were no other people around. Jonah was a major event. She just wished they wouldn't be so obvious about it.

Most of them were just staring, but Heather and Courtney were giggling, acting like they'd just come face to face with Leonardo DiCaprio. Well, Jonah *was* good-looking, there was no question about that. But the boys were gaping, too. And some of them weren't acting very friendly.

Kyle Bailey, who considered himself a real tough guy, made no effort to conceal his mistrust. "You gotta remember *something*, man."

Donna broke in. "His name is Jonah, not 'man.' He has selective amnesia. That's all he remembers."

"Yeah, so he says," Kyle muttered. He moved around Jonah, as if he expected to find a clue to Jonah's real identity on the back of his head. When he didn't find any answers, he said, "I'll go get Travis."

"Selective amnesia," Mike Salicki said. "I never heard of that."

Big surprise, Donna thought. Mike wasn't exactly a mental giant.

"Yeah," Carlos Guzman echoed. "Sounds pretty bogus to me."

"Bogus," Jonah repeated.

"Don't you know what that means?" Heather asked him.

He seemed to be concentrating. " 'Sham,' " he pronounced. " 'Counterfeit, fake, spurious.' "

"Aha!" Mike declared triumphantly.

Donna looked at him in annoyance. "What's *that* supposed to mean?"

"For crying out loud, Donna, he's got a memory. He sounds like he's quoting from a dictionary!"

"I do?" Jonah said with interest. He didn't try to defend himself. Maura appeared by his side with a cup of soup. He took a sip. "This is good," he said appreciatively. "I haven't eaten in a while."

"Aha!" Mike cried out again.

Donna was getting seriously irritated. "*Now* what?"

"He remembers that he hasn't had anything to eat!"

"I know that I feel hungry," Jonah said. "Wouldn't that mean I haven't eaten in some time?"

Kyle reappeared with Travis. "What's going on?" Travis asked abruptly.

"I found him on the Verrazano Bridge," Donna said. "He has amnesia." Travis glanced at her, and she thought he was about to ask her what she was doing on the Verrazano Bridge. But then his gaze returned to Jonah. A mysterious stranger took precedence over any annoyance he might feel with his girlfriend.

"Jonah, this is Travis," Donna said.

"Our leader," Maura chimed in.

Jonah rose from his chair and made a little bow with his head. "I am honored to meet you."

Donna thought Travis would like that, but instead he looked at Jonah with undisguised suspicion all over his face. "You didn't come from around here," he stated flatly.

"How do you know that?" Jonah asked.

"The way you talk," Travis said. "You don't have a New York accent. But you didn't come here from very far away."

"How do you know that?" Jonah repeated.

"Your shoes. They're clean, you couldn't have been walking for a long time."

"Good grief, Travis, give him a break," Donna remark. "You don't have to put Jonah on trial."

Donna realized immediately what a stupid comment that was for her to make, and the fierce look

Travis shot her confirmed it. Travis did *not* like to be contradicted in public. He wasn't that crazy about being criticized in private either. She tried to make up for it with a humble question that acknowledged his authority. "Can he stay here in the Community with us, Travis?"

Travis studied Jonah for a moment. "I want to meet with my executive committee." He nodded toward Mike and Carlos. Carlos let out a groan.

"Another meeting? We were meeting all morning! We were going to play some basketball."

"A crisis in the Community takes precedence over playing basketball," Travis stated.

"Am I a crisis?" Jonah asked as Mike and Carlos got up and joined their leader. Travis glanced at him witheringly, and didn't reply.

"Should we put him under room arrest until we decide about him?" Mike asked Travis.

Donna couldn't restrain herself. She went over to Travis and spoke softly, so Jonah couldn't hear her. "That's ridiculous," she fumed. "He hasn't done anything wrong! Look at him!"

Travis raised his eyebrows. "You think he looks normal?"

Donna glanced back at the man, who bore a remote resemblance to the pictures of Jesus in the Sunday School Bible storybooks she'd read as a child. "Well, he doesn't look *dangerous*."

Travis looked back at Jonah again. "Okay, we won't put him under arrest. But you're responsible for him, so keep an eye on him." With that, he left the lobby with Carlos and Mike.

Donna had won, but she was still feeling a little miffed. She didn't like Travis giving her orders like that, especially right in front of Carlos and Mike.

And if he actually thought Jonah could be dangerous, why was he putting his girlfriend in jeopardy?

She looked over at Jonah, and her heart melted. The poor guy was still getting bombarded by questions, and Maura was flirting outrageously. He seemed about as dangerous as a flea. She went back to the group and took over.

"Okay, folks, leave him alone," she said briskly. "I'm sure he's tired." She managed to extract Jonah from the crowd, and started to take him toward the elevator. "You can lie down in my room," she told him.

"Actually, I am not tired," he said. "Could we perhaps go out and take a walk?"

"That's a good idea," Donna said. "Maybe you'll see something that triggers your memory. That's what happened on my soap opera, you know. The guy who had amnesia, he saw his childhood home and everything came back to him."

Jonah smiled and nodded, but she got the feeling he had no idea what she was talking about. The guard at the door wanted to know where they were going. Donna considered her options, and decided to start off by giving Jonah an overall view of New York.

Jonah looked around with interest as Donna led him into the lobby of the World Trade towers. "I haven't been to the Observation Deck in ages," she told him. She was relieved when the elevator button lit up. "You know, it's weird how all the electricity still works, when there's no one to run it," she said. "Elevators run, street lights come on automatically, the plumbing works, too. Don't you think that's strange?"

On the way to the towers, Donna had explained

about Disappearance Day. Jonah hadn't seemed terribly alarmed. What she was telling him now didn't appear to intrigue him either. "For me, everything is strange," he said.

"Well, I'm glad this elevator's working," she said. "Otherwise we'd be walking up more than a hundred stories." Still, she experienced a little shiver of apprehension when the doors opened and they stepped into the elevator. What if the electricity stopped working while they were in here? On the other hand, there would be worse people to be trapped in an elevator with than Jonah.

She liked him. He hadn't said much on the way there, but he'd listened to her in a way no one ever seemed to listen to her—seriously, and with interest. And despite his predicament, he was calm and gentle. It was contagious—Donna could feel all her pent-up tension draining out of her.

"You're lucky you found the Community," she told him now. "Travis wants us to become a real society and start a whole new civilization."

"Is this good?"

Donna hesitated. She didn't want to be disloyal, but there was something about Jonah's penetrating gaze that made her want to confide in him. "I think Travis is a little too ambitious," she admitted. "He's pretty strict with himself, and he expects a lot from other people."

"Is this bad?"

"They just don't want to work that hard. But it's a nice place, the Community," she added quickly. "You'll like it there. It's certainly better than being alone."

"Is there another place?"

"Well, there are the so-called rebels across the

street, but there are only eight of them. I think you're better off with us.''

"Why?"

"They just can't deal with what happened,'' Donna sighed. "They think that all the people who disappeared are still alive, and there must be a way to get them back. They won't accept the fact that they're gone forever.''

"*Is* it a fact?'' Jonah asked.

Donna looked at him sharply. "Don't let Travis hear you say that,'' she warned him.

"I won't,'' he said. "I say this only to you.''

She felt like blushing. "Why me?''

"I don't know.''

"Maybe we knew each other before,'' Donna said. "No, that's not possible. I'd remember you.'' They stepped out onto the Promenade atop the Observation Deck. "This is the highest outdoor viewing platform in the world,'' she told him. She watched his face as he looked out at the city of New York.

"What is that?'' he asked, pointing.

"The Empire State Building. Before the World Trade Center was built, that was the tallest building in the city. There's a building taller than this one in Chicago, but I'll bet that someday we'll have a building even taller than that right here in New York.''

"How?'' he asked. "Who will build it?''

She was silent.

"You are sad,'' he observed.

"It's just that sometimes I forget it's only us now,'' she said.

*　　*　　*

"He's so *sweet*," she told Travis later at dinner.

"What did you find out about him?"

"There's nothing to find out," she said. "He has amnesia, remember?"

"He *says* he has amnesia," Travis noted.

"Why would he lie?"

Travis shook his head wearily. "Donna, you can be so naive. We don't know what this guy's agenda is. He could be an emissary from some other community that we don't know anything about. He could be a spy, he could be looking for worlds to conquer."

"Yeah, well, if you're going to look at all possibilities, he could be an alien."

Travis frowned. "This isn't a joking matter, Donna. I have to protect this community."

Donna sighed. "Travis, I spent practically the whole day with him. He's no Attila the Hun. He's sweet, and gentle, and innocent. He's almost like a child sometimes."

"He's not a child, he's a man," Travis said. "I don't trust him. And neither should you. Don't forget, everything you say and do reflects on me."

Donna tried to keep her tone light, but she couldn't prevent a defensive note from slipping into her response. "Travis, I'm a person, not just your girlfriend. I'm entitled to my own opinion, aren't I?"

He said nothing in response, but the look he gave her wasn't reassuring.

Kesha was wearing soft-soled tennis shoes, but a footstep in any kind of shoe was bound to make a noise on these silent streets. She remained two full blocks behind Martina as she followed her downtown. She stayed close to the buildings, so she could duck into a doorway if Martina happened to turn around.

She felt ridiculous, like some sort of sleazy private investigator, tailing her friend down Broadway. Espionage wasn't a particular interest of hers, and she'd never been much of a Nancy Drew fan.

But there was a real mystery going on, and she was worried. Every day, just as the sun was about to set, Martina left the health club. She would return about an hour later, looking suspiciously spacy and out-of-it. When Kesha asked her where she'd been, she'd mumble something like "out for a walk," and then retreat to her little yoga room.

This wasn't like Martina. Over the past month, Kesha felt like she'd come to know her pretty well. Martina was outgoing, friendly and spirited. Kesha had once sat next to the twin sister, Rosa, in a class, and she remembered Rosa being like that too. Warm, easy to be with, comfortable. They both laughed a lot, and they didn't seem to have any deep, dark secrets. And no one ever would have accused either of the Santiago sisters of being aggressive.

They weren't wild either. But now, when she returned from these strange outings, Martina bore an odd scent, a smell Kesha couldn't identify. Alcohol? Something else? When she spoke, her words were slurred. And she barely spoke at all. Something was very, very wrong.

And since Kesha knew it was highly unlikely any of the other rebels would notice Martina's behavior or become concerned, she had to take matters into her own hands. So here she was, sneaking up behind her like some sort of half-baked spy.

They were on the stretch of Broadway where she and Donna used to hunt down vintage clothes, but she didn't look in any of the windows. She kept her eyes focused on the small dark-haired figure walking two blocks in front of her. Martina wasn't looking in any store windows either, and even from a distance Kesha could see that she wasn't just out for a walk—Martina was walking with the kind of determination that made it clear she had a direction, a place to be.

After a while, Kesha noticed that the stores had changed. There were dead, lacquered ducks hanging in the windows, and Chinese words above the doors. They were obviously in Chinatown now. Kesha was confused. What was Martina doing down here? Had she developed some sort of constant craving for egg rolls?

When she saw Martina turn left on a small side street, she quickened her pace. Afraid she was going to lose her, she broke into a light jog, and she was panting by the time she reached the corner. It was good that she had started running, though, or she would have missed Martina going into a narrow, gray stone building.

She paused to catch her breath, and then walked over there. From the outside, it was a nondescript building. There were no signs indicating what lay within . . . no, wait, there was something, a small glass-enclosed square of paper just beside the door frame. Kesha went up the stone steps and looked at it closely. *Mystic Herbal Connections. 2nd floor.*

She opened the door and crept quietly but quickly up the stairs. She found the door labeled *Mystic Herbal Connections* and touched the doorknob. It opened easily.

She found herself in what looked like a waiting room. There was a scratched metal desk, and two threadbare sofas facing a coffee table. There was another door, which she guessed led to another room. She paused, but she heard nothing coming from beyond the door.

There were some papers on the coffee table. She tiptoed over and picked one up. "Mystic Herbal Connections," she read silently. "Utilize the power of ancient herbal remedies to achieve a communication beyond this earthly world. Find loved ones, exchange messages, and establish a connection which transcends your physical state."

It was then that she caught a whiff of something. A wisp of smoke floated through the room. It was a strange smell, but a familiar one, and it seemed to be coming from the space under the closed door.

Kesha edged closer to the door, and pressed her ear against it. She couldn't hear anything, but the smell was stronger. Gently, very gently, she pushed on the door.

Beyond the door there was darkness, with a tiny illumination, a spark of light near the floor. She could recognize the smell now—it was the scent that followed Martina back to the health club every day. And then she heard Martina's voice, very soft and dreamy.

"Rosa, Rosa . . . can you hear me? Are you there?" Then, after a moment, "Yes, I feel you now, you're here in me."

Kesha's eyes had become adjusted to the darkness now, and she could see more. The illumination came from a bowl on the floor. Something was burning inside it. Martina was on her knees, bent over the bowl. Her eyes were closed, and she was breathing in the fumes deeply.

"Martina?"

There was no response. Now, she began swaying side to side, chanting tunelessly.

"Martina?" Kesha spoke louder this time.

Slowly, Martina turned her head toward her. By now, Kesha was getting the full impact of the scent that emanated from the bowl. Her head was spinning. In a few seconds, she'd be completely dizzy.

"Martina, let's get out of here."

Martina's voice was weak. "My sister . . ."

"She's not here."

"Rosa?" Martina called plaintively.

Was she drunk? Stoned? Hallucinating? Kesha steeled herself and tried to sound stern. "Martina, come with me," she ordered. "We'll find Rosa."

Martina didn't move. Holding her breath, Kesha moved closer. She put a hand on Martina's arm. Martina didn't struggle. She allowed herself to be lifted to an upright position and led out of the room. In the waiting area, her eyes cleared somewhat.

She gazed up at Kesha in desperation. "Did you mean that? Can we find Rosa?"

Kesha nodded. "Yes, I guarantee it. We'll find Rosa. Now let's go." She knew she was behaving very aggressively. She didn't care.

In her dream, Ashley had hair again. Her soft curls floated in the wind. She was running, running . . . running to Corey . . . Corey would save her, Corey always saved her. But why wasn't he coming to get her? Why did he just stand there, way off in the distance, waiting for her?

Maybe it was the frustration that woke her. Or maybe the fact that it was only nine o'clock in the evening had something to do with it. In any case, Ashley was awake, and she knew she wouldn't be falling asleep again any time soon.

This was getting aggravating. She knew it was Corey in the dream, she was positive now. She could see his face. Corey was appearing in her subconscious because he wanted to rescue her.

But rescue her from what? Corey had disappeared, along with everyone else on earth. She was the lucky one, still here in the real world. This dream made no sense at all.

She got off the bed and went to her vanity table, where she examined her scalp. Some hair was beginning to grow back, but it looked more like fuzz than hair. She didn't like it, so she picked up a razor to shave her head. Then she stopped.

Maybe she wasn't so lucky. Maybe what she thought was the real world wasn't the real world at all. Corey, and everyone else, could be in the real world, while the seniors from Madison High were trapped in some sort of alternate universe . . .

No, this was stupid. And why was she making such a fuss about figuring out a meaning for this dream? It was just a dream, for crying out loud. It didn't have to mean anything at all.

She had to get out of that room. And she was hungry, too. Maybe she could find someone who hadn't had dinner yet. They could go out and look for a restaurant that still had stuff in a freezer and a microwave . . .

There was a frantic knocking on her door, followed by a frantic voice. "Ashley? Ashley, are you in there?"

She got up and opened the door. Maura stood there and her eyes were bright with excitement. "Ashley, come quick! You have to see this!"

"Wait a sec." Ashley stuck her bare feet into some clogs, and came out into the hall. "What's going on?"

"Travis and Donna are having this major battle!"

Ashley stopped. "And what makes you think I want to see that?"

"Come on, Ashley, how much drama do we get around here?"

Maura had a point. Ashley followed her down the stairs. "What are they fighting about?"

"Jonah."

Ashley hadn't seen much of the newcomer since he'd arrived. He'd been pretty inconspicuous, and he didn't seem to be much of a talker. Donna had taken him under her wing, and they always seemed to be together.

The battle between Travis and Donna was taking place publicly, a situation that seemed extremely strange to Ashley. Travis had always impressed her as a man of discretion, very much aware of his public image. He was the consummate political type, who displayed a calm and confident exterior face that gave nothing away in regard to his real feelings, if he had any.

He certainly had some feelings now, and he was making no attempt to hide them. His eyes were burning as he spoke to Donna and Jonah, who stood a little to one side. "Then you admit you were conspiring behind my back."

"Travis, we were exchanging ideas, that's all!" Donna protested. "No one was conspiring. Mike, you were there, tell Travis what we were doing.''

Mike Salicki shrugged. ''I don't know, you two were looking pretty cozy to me.'' Donna glared at him fiercely, but Mike didn't back down.

Travis's attention was focused on Jonah. ''Now I don't know who you are or what you want—''

''Neither does he,'' Donna interrupted with a smile, but her attempt at humor didn't go over well with Travis.

''Shut up!'' he barked at her. Donna drew in her breath sharply and stepped backward. More kids had gathered, and the atmosphere was tense. Donna's cheeks were flaming.

Ashley glanced at Maura. It was very clear that Maura was observing all this with delight. That wasn't really a surprise—Maura was always coming on to Travis. But she was rather appalled to see Maura taking so much pleasure in another girl's embarrassment.

And now Travis's eyes were fixed on Donna, and his voice was like steel. ''You betrayed me,'' he said.

''Travis, no, that's not true!'' Donna cried out in bewilderment. ''We were just talking—''

''Scheming,'' Travis corrected her.

''No! Jonah, tell him what we've been doing.''

Jonah spoke. ''Donna has been very, very good to me.''

Ashley felt sure he was speaking innocently, but it didn't come out that way. And it certainly didn't pacify Travis. He turned the full force of his fury on the man dressed in white.

''So that's it,'' he said. ''You want *her*.''

''Oh, Travis,'' Donna moaned, but he wouldn't let her continue.

"Get out of here," he said through clenched teeth. "Get out of this building. I don't want to see your face again."

"Travis, you can't do that," Donna pleaded. "He's alone, he doesn't know the city, he won't be able to survive on his own."

"He won't be alone," Travis stated. "You're going with him."

Ashley had never seen a blush fade so rapidly from anyone's cheeks. Donna was now completely white. "Travis . . ." she whispered.

"Get out!"

I can't let this happen, Ashley thought wildly. *They can't be banished like this, it isn't right.* She knew nothing about the stranger, but Donna was sweet and childlike; she needed her friends around, she needed a community. She wanted to say something, to add her own voice in protest—but she couldn't. Travis was now gazing around the room as if daring any of the observers to contradict him, and none of them was on the verge of doing so. His guards, his so-called buddies, were drawing closer to him, forming a line of protection and defense. If Ashley opened her mouth, he'd only banish her, too. And she was too scared to put herself in that position.

So with shame at her own cowardice, and fear for Donna, she watched as Travis's buddies escorted the two infidels to the hotel door, flung it open, and threw them out.

when they reached the steps outside the mystic herbal place, Martina was still a little wobbly. She had to clutch Kesha's arm as she walked down the steps to the sidewalk. Kesha wasn't surprised that Martina was so feeble. She had a headache herself, but by holding her breath inside she'd managed to avoid the worst effects of the herbs.

"Take deep breaths," Kesha commanded, and Martina attempted to obey, but her breathing was more like a series of gasps.

Kesha kept a grip on her as she coughed. "Slow down! What was that stuff you were burning in there, anyway? Marijuana?"

Donna was finally able to speak, though her voice was thin. "No, nothing like that. It was just a special mix of herbs and incense and spices. All natural stuff."

"Marijuana is natural stuff," Kesha pointed out.

"This mixture isn't supposed to get you high," Donna told her. "I got the recipe from a book on Eastern remedies."

"Remedies?" Kesha looked at her skeptically. "You mean, that stuff is supposed to be medical?"

"Not exactly. Breathing special combinations of herbs is supposed to help you in certain ways."

"What kind of ways?"

Martina paused. She started walking, and studied the pavement with unusual intensity. When she finally spoke, she sounded more than a little abashed. "Oh . . . supposedly, you can look into your past lives, or see the future, or communicate with the dead."

Kesha groaned. "Oh, for crying out loud, Martina. You're a sensible person. Don't tell me you really believe that stuff."

Martina gave her an embarrassed smile. "Didn't you ever see that Woody Allen movie, where Mia Farrow goes to a Chinese doctor, and he gives her herbs that make all sorts of weird things happen? Like, she became invisible from some herbs, and she brought back a dead friend."

"No, but I'll bet it was supposed to be a fantasy."

"Yeah, maybe . . . but I was ready to try anything."

"For what? What were you trying to do? Get into a past life?"

"Oh, Kesha, get real. You have to know what I was trying to do."

Kesha knew. "You wanted to reach your sister."

Martina nodded. "She's alive, Kesha. I know, I've said that a million times, and you keep telling me it's just wishful thinking. But you said yourself, I'm a sensible person. I'm not crazy. I feel her." She stopped walking, and faced Kesha squarely. "Do you believe me?"

Kesha didn't want to. But she nodded anyway, because maybe, against her better judgment, she did.

"Then help me," Martina pleaded. "You said you would."

Kesha nodded again. "I will. But you have to do your part."

"What do you mean?"

"We have to get out of that health club, we have to move on. If we go up to Central Park, maybe we can find some clues about what really happened. You have to help me convince the others."

To her amazement and gratification, Martina nodded. "I will. I'm realizing that it's not enough to make mental contact, I have to get physically closer to her. And the only way I'll get her back—the only way we'll get everyone back—is if we can figure out where they are, why they're gone, who took them."

Kesha couldn't say anything right away. She knew now that she had an ally, and that was good. Martina would stand by her in her next confrontation with Jake.

But as pleased as Kesha was that Martina was siding with her, she still had trouble with her reasons. This idea that all the people on earth had been taken away by some power—that wasn't an easy notion for Kesha to buy into. Kesha had never been a New Ager, she'd never had any interest in ESP or unexplained phenomena or any of that occult stuff. She didn't even like *The X-Files*. She had no belief in psychics, fortune tellers, or palm readers.

But if Martina was willing to help her get the rebels out of the health club, Kesha had to go along with her. And maybe, just maybe, Martina's ideas weren't all that bizarre.

Suddenly, Martina clutched her arm. "Kesha, look!"

Kesha was almost afraid to. Had Martina suddenly spotted an extraterrestrial biological entity or something?

But no, Martina was staring into the window of a Chinese grocery store. "Kesha, there've got to be noodles and interesting sauces in there. Let's check it out! I am so sick of soup out of a can!"

They returned to the health club with bags full of exotic Chinese food. It was completely dark out by now, but Martina had good eyes. She stopped. "Someone's there."

Kesha stopped. "Are you trying to freak me out?" She tried to sound unconcerned, but she could hear the slight quiver in her own voice. But Martina had moved on and left her behind. "Who's there?" she called.

Then the mystery people stepped under a street light, and now Kesha could identify them. One was Donna. The other was a man, dressed in white. Kesha had never seen him before. She stood still and listened.

"Martina!"

"Donna, hi . . ."

"This is Jonah."

"Jonah?"

"I found him. On the Verrazano Bridge."

Then a soft, deep voice spoke. "Hello, Martina. It's a pleasure to meet you."

There was a moment of silence, before Martina said, "Yeah, me too . . . Kesha? Look who's here."

Reluctantly, Kesha stepped into the light.

"Kesha, hi! This is Jonah."

"Hello, Kesha," said the man.

Kesha nodded in response.

"How's everything going over at the Community?" Martina asked Donna.

"Not so great," Donna said. "Travis threw us out."

Martina gasped. "What? Why would he do that? What happened?" She was looking at Jonah as she asked, but Donna answered.

"Travis doesn't trust him. See, Jonah has amnesia, he doesn't know where he came from. Travis thinks he's just faking it, that he's from another group who wants to take over the Community."

"Why did he throw *you* out?" Kesha wanted to know.

"He thinks I'm plotting with Jonah. Or he thinks there's something going on between me and Jonah. Or maybe he just doesn't love me anymore. In any case, we're on our own." Kesha didn't miss the tremor in her ex-friend's voice.

"I can't believe Travis would do that," Martina marveled.

"I can," Kesha stated. "He's always been a jerk. Now he's a paranoid jerk."

"He's not paranoid," Donna piped up. "He's—he's under a lot of pressure. That's all. He's probably regretting what he did right now."

Kesha was floored. "I can't believe you're still defending him!"

"You just don't really know him," Donna said.

"Thank goodness," Kesha retorted.

Martina spoke up hastily. "Whatever. The question is, what are you going to do now?"

"I don't know," Donna said. "It's sort of scary."

"You can stay with us," Martina said. "Here, at the health club."

Donna hesitated. "I feel sort of strange doing that. I mean, I don't know if I want to join the rebels . . ."

Kesha made a disparaging noise. "What's wrong, are you afraid Travis might get mad at you?"

"You don't have to join us," Martina said. "But you shouldn't go wandering around tonight looking for a place to stay. You're all shaken up, and it's dark. We have plenty of space."

"That might be a good idea," Jonah said to Donna.

"Okay," Donna agreed.

"C'mon in," Martina said, "I'll take you to see Jake," and started to lead them to the door.

"Martina?" Kesha said. "Can I speak to you for a minute? Out here?"

"Sure." To Donna, she said, "You guys go on in, I'll be there in a second."

Kesha waited until she was sure Donna and Jonah couldn't hear her. "Martina, are you sure we should let them inside?"

"Why not?" Martina asked.

"Well, they could be spies for the other side."

"Good grief, Kesha, we're not at war."

Kesha shook her head. "I just don't feel comfortable with this."

"We can't abandon them," Martina stated. "Donna's your friend, Kesha, remember?"

"Was," Kesha corrected. "And what about this Jonah person? Who is he, where did he come from? Did he just pop up out of nowhere? This amnesia business . . . that's only on TV, I've never heard of anyone having amnesia in real life."

"Kesha, just because you never heard of it

doesn't mean it can't exist," Martina argued. "And we've all said many times that it's hard to believe we're the only people left on earth. There could be other groups like ours, and he could be coming from one of them. Or he could have been on his own the past month, poor guy."

"I don't like his looks," Kesha muttered.

"Then don't marry him," Martina said good-naturedly. "Come on, it's getting cold out here."

They found Donna and Jonah in the snack bar with Jake and Adam. Donna was telling her story. Adam listened with his mouth open, and occasionally said, "Wow." Jake wasn't speaking at all. But for the first time in a long while, Kesha detected a spark of interest in his face. This was encouraging.

But when Jake finally spoke, she was disappointed. His first question had nothing at all to do with Jonah or the situation. "How is everyone in the Community?" he asked Donna.

"Everyone?" Donna asked. A small smile appeared on her sad face. "Or someone in particular?"

Jonah studied Jake with interest.

Under his gaze, Jake gave a nonchalant shrug. "There was a girl."

"Ashley," Donna told Jonah. "You met her. They used to be together."

Once again, Jake shrugged, but this time it was totally unconvincing. "It's over. I gotta deal with it."

"Good!" Kesha said with approval. "Finally, Jake, you're talking sense. It's about time. Forget about her and get on with your life."

Donna turned to face her. "How can you talk to him like that? How can you be so callous? Do you have any idea what it's like to be dumped by some-one you love?'' Her eyes welled up with tears.

"Love," Jonah repeated.

Donna brushed the tears from her eyes. "Do you remember love?"

There were furrows on Jonah's brow, but he nodded. "Love is a feeling."

Jake agreed appreciatively. "No kidding."

Kesha rolled her eyes. "Give me a break." She felt in desperate need of fresh air. She left the snack bar and went back outside.

But she wasn't alone out there. A small figure was standing close to the door. "Shalini?"

"Hi, Kesha."

"What are you doing out here by yourself?"

"Alex and I are going to the movies."

"Oh." That was one of their regular outings. Alex knew how to run a real movie projector, and they liked to sit alone in theaters and watch movies on a big screen. Kesha wouldn't have minded go-ing along with them sometime. Watching video movies on TV wasn't the same as watching movies on a real screen. But Alex never invited anyone else to go with them.

"But he thinks I should wear a jacket," Shalini continued. "So he went back in to get me one."

"Oh. What are you going to see?"

" 'Deadly Demon Surfers on Mars.' " She shud-dered. "I hope it's not too scary."

"You don't like horror movies?"

"No. I get terrible nightmares."

"Then why are you going to see it?"

"Alex loves movies like that."

Kesha gazed at her curiously. "Do you always do what he wants to do?"

Shalini smiled, but she didn't answer. Kesha persisted. "Why do you let him order you around?"

She thought Shalini would tell her to mind her own business, which she had every right to say, but instead, Shalini seemed to actually consider the question. "He feels so powerless," she told Kesha. "If I let him make decisions like this, he can feel he has some sort of control of his life."

This wasn't what Kesha expected to hear. "But what about you? What do you get out of this?"

"He watches out for me," she said simply. "So I don't feel so lonely and sad."

Kesha didn't know what to say. She'd always assumed that loners like Shalini were loners by choice, because they didn't want to make friends. She knew she was getting very personal with someone she barely knew, but she couldn't resist. "Are you guys in love?"

She couldn't see Shalini blush in the darkness, but she had no doubt that the girl was embarrassed by the question. "I don't know," she said. "I've never been in love before. What does it feel like?"

Kesha couldn't answer that. She'd never been in love herself. At least, she didn't think she had. She did know that she'd never had a boyfriend. Donna used to tell her she needed to tone down if she ever wanted to attract a guy, that her aggressive nature turned guys off. But what did Donna know? Personally, Kesha preferred to wait until she met a guy who could treat her as an equal. Apparently, all girls, like Shalini, didn't share her feelings.

Alex appeared at that moment with a sweater for Shalini. "Put this on," he ordered her, and Shalini meekly obliged.

"Bye, Kesha," she whispered, and they disappeared into the night.

Kesha remained alone outside for a few more minutes. She didn't feel like going to her room or rejoining the conversation in the snack bar. When the door opened and David Chu came out, she was almost glad to see him. She actually managed something that vaguely resembled a smile.

"Hi, David, what's up?"

He seemed pleased that she actually was speaking to him. "Not much, what's up with you?"

"Not much." Geez, what a deadly conversation.

"Wanna party?" he asked.

"What did you have in mind?" she asked cautiously.

"Let's do some bar hopping," he suggested. "Hey, how about this? We could hit twenty different bars and try twenty different brands of beer and choose the one we like best. We could rank them, make a contest out of it."

"I don't like beer," Kesha said.

"So . . . so we can try twenty vodkas." He grinned, and she had to admit, in all objectivity, that he had a dazzling smile. Kesha had never understood what so many girls found attractive about David, but the smile and the eye contact he was making gave her a hint.

But she wasn't about to fall victim to his charms. "I don't drink, David."

"Oh." His face fell. "Nobody around here wants to have any fun."

"We have better things to do, David," she said, trying to sound stern.

"Like what?"

She had no answer for that.

David gazed across the street at the hotel. "I wonder what's going on over there."

"You could always go back there and find out," Kesha said. She was being nasty, she knew that, but she couldn't help herself. It had been an annoying day, and David was a pain.

"Yeah, maybe I will."

"David, I didn't mean that," Kesha said hastily. "You can't leave the rebels."

"No? Why not?"

"Because—because we're already in the minority, we can't afford to lose anyone. Besides, you'd be miserable in the Community with Travis's rules and regulations."

"Yeah, well, I'm not having any fun here. At least there are some girls over there. No offense, but you won't hang out, I can't go near Shalini, and Martina hates my guts."

He had a point. Kesha couldn't argue that.

"No party animal could survive here," he said, and ambled off into the darkness. Kesha didn't try to stop him.

So now the rebels were down to seven. Then she remembered that they had Donna and the mysterious Jonah now, which made them nine, but that was no comfort. Hopefully, they wouldn't be here long. Donna couldn't be trusted, she'd proved that a month ago. As for this Jonah . . . maybe she was being as paranoid as Travis, but she didn't trust him either.

Ashley couldn't sleep. She'd been doing nothing *but* sleeping lately, but this time, when she actually wanted to sleep, she couldn't do it. It was three in the morning, and she was wide awake.

She wanted to have that dream again, the dream

about Corey. She had to reach him, to talk to him, she had to find out what he wanted to tell her.

Even as these thoughts passed through her mind, she felt confused and fairly ridiculous. Back in her modeling days, she'd known a couple of girls who were seriously into dreams, tarot cards, astrology. When she heard them talking about it, she felt a little embarrassed for them. And at the same time, she felt envy. She wished she could believe in something that would provide her with answers.

But she wasn't going to get any answers tonight. Her eyes were open and her mind felt absurdly alert for this hour. Maybe it was the image of Donna's frightened face when Travis threw the two of them out that kept her awake. Maybe it was guilt at her own lack of effort to help Donna. Whatever the reason, there was no way she could sleep.

So she got out of bed, turned on the light, and looked in her bookcase for something to read. But nothing appealed to her. She didn't want anything boring, but she didn't want anything too interesting either, or she'd never sleep.

She turned to the small video collection she'd gathered over the weeks. There wasn't anything new, but she picked a comedy she thought she wouldn't mind watching again. She turned on the TV, and waited until the screen displayed the usual fuzz. Then she inserted the tape into the VCR, and pressed PLAY. Nothing happened. She pressed PLAY again, and wondered if the button was stuck. It wasn't a big deal; she could always go out tomorrow and pick up another one from the closest Radio Shack or Circuit City. But she'd have to find something else to do now.

And then, her eye was caught by something on the screen. There was a change in the fuzzy pattern. It seemed to be getting darker—no, not darker. The fuzziness was fading, that's what was different. The screen was becoming blank. She watched it with mild curiosity. There must be some sort of electric current in the air affecting the antennas. Was there lightning? She was about to go to the window to look out, but her eyes wouldn't leave the TV screen. She was transfixed.

Because now something else was happening. In the blankness of the screen, an image was forming. It was all shadows at first, but slowly, slowly, a shape was emerging. A face . . . the face of a man.

It was Corey.

Ashley put a hand to her mouth, suppressing a silent scream. Was she dreaming that she was awake and looking at the TV? Had she lost her mind?

She moved closer to the set. It was definitely Corey. He was wearing the tortoiseshell glasses he always wore, and he was dressed as he was usually dressed, as he was dressed in her dreams, in jeans and a light blue shirt.

"Corey?" she whispered.

Did she really expect an image on a TV screen to respond? Corey didn't speak. But his lips were moving. She crept closer.

Yes, the lips were moving, and they seemed to be forming the same word, again and again. She tried to imitate the movement with her own lips.

Help. Help. That's what he was saying. Help. He was calling for help.

And then it hit her. He wasn't coming to save her. He was asking her to rescue him.

From the journal of Jake Robbins:

I haven't jogged or worked out in a while. I've actually had other things to do.

David Chu left us three days ago. I don't think it's a problem. He wasn't much of a rebel and he only wants to hit on girls. On the up side, we have two new people here—Donna, and a man she found wandering around, Jonah. He's pretty interesting. He doesn't say much, but he's a good listener. There's something very calm and peaceful about him. And even though he's quiet, he seems wise. He knows something, and I think I can learn from him. Just being around him makes me feel better. He doesn't criticize me. He looks interested in everything I say. I have this idea that maybe he actually respects me. I'm starting to think maybe I can be a real leader. I feel like I'm waking up, like I'm losing the blues.

I haven't been thinking so much about Ashley.

"What's the deal?" Kesha asked Martina. "Are they setting up permanent residence here or what?"

Martina looked up from her book. "What?"

"Donna and what's-his-face, Jonah. It's been three days since they showed up and they're still here."

"So what?"

"So—so, so nothing." Kesha paced the room. "I have to get out of here. *We* have to get out of here."

Martina put the book down. "Yeah, I know. And I tried to talk to Jake about moving on, I told you that. He said he wanted to talk to Jonah."

"Jonah! What does Jonah know about anything?"

"I haven't the slightest idea. But Jake thinks a lot of him. So does Donna."

"I don't get it," Kesha said. "Okay, Jonah's older. But that doesn't make him any smarter. For crying out loud, he doesn't say anything and they're acting like he's some sort of wise man!"

"I know," Martina agreed. "But look on the bright side of this. At least Jake isn't moping and acting like a space cadet. And have you noticed that Donna isn't going on and on crying over Travis?"

"I haven't paid any attention to Donna at all," Kesha said stiffly. She paced the yoga room. "I can't take this anymore," she declared. "Come on, let's go confront Jake together. Do you know where he is?"

"Wherever Jonah is, I guess," Martina replied.

They found them in the game room. Jonah was watching as Jake and Adam played pool.

"Watch it," Adam was yelling. "Here comes the hustler." He aimed his cue and struck a ball. It rolled into the middle of the table and sat there.

"Brilliant," Jake crowed. "Now, watch the destroyer." He used his cue to do something that Kesha assumed was good, since it was greeted with a groan from Adam.

"Jake, we want to talk to you," Martina said.

"Sure," Jake replied, taking aim again. "Talk."

Martina and Kesha exchanged looks. This wasn't the time or the place. But before either of them could propose anything, Jonah spoke unexpectedly.

"I want to talk to *you*, Kesha."

Kesha looked at him in surprise. "About what?" she asked.

"About Donna."

Kesha stared at him. "Why?"

"She tells me you were friends. Now you are no longer friends. Why is that?"

His language skills had certainly improved, Kesha thought. Enough so that he was now asking personal questions.

"None of your business," Kesha replied.

"Kesha," Jake said, "he just wants to help. I know you and Donna have had problems, but you need to work them out. We have to stick together. You guys have to make up."

Kesha glared at him. "This isn't your business either!"

"It is my business," Jake stated. "You guys made me the leader here, remember? That makes me responsible for everyone's welfare."

Kesha's mouth fell open. Since when did Jake care about anyone's welfare but his own? Her annoyance flared up.

"Some leader you are," she accused him. "You couldn't lead a bear into the woods."

"Kesha," Martina chided her, but Kesha didn't care. She wanted to hurt his feelings. Her voice rose.

"The world has practically come to an end and you're playing pool! Are we just going to sit in this stupid building till we die of old age? Or disappear like everyone else? If you can't be a leader, Jake, turn the position over to me and *I'll* lead us out of here!"

Her voice had risen to a shriek. Jake was speechless. *No one* was speaking. There was no telling how long they all would have remained silent if Cam hadn't walked in.

"Jake?"

Everyone whirled around and faced Cam. He stepped back in alarm. "Hey, don't kill the messenger!"

"What are you talking about?" Jake asked irritably.

"You're not going to be happy to hear this," Cam said. "David Chu's here, downstairs."

Jake let out a loud, long groan. "What does he want?"

"He say he wants to come back and join us. He doesn't like living at the Community."

"Yeah, well, too bad," Jake said. "He made his bed, now he has to lie in it. We don't want him back here."

"Why?" Jonah asked.

"You don't know him," Jake said. "The guy's got nothing going for him. He thinks he's a playboy and a party animal, and he won't take anything seriously. He's basically worthless."

"This is true," Martina piped up. "He's a pig, he treats people like dirt. I'm with you, Jake. Don't let him back in."

Jonah gazed at her. "Because of your sister?"

Martina gaped. "How did you know that?"

"Donna informed me." He turned to Jake. "Surely, he couldn't be totally worthless, Jake. Everything that lives has value."

Now everyone was looking at Jonah. This was more than he'd ever said to any of them before.

"Oh, yeah?" Kesha asked. "How about roaches?"

"Come on, Kesha," Jake urged. "Give him a break."

"Thank you," Jonah said to Jake. "Could you give David a break too?"

Jake looked torn.

"Hey!" Kesha cried in outrage. "Who do you think you are, Jonah? You walk in here, a total stranger, and start telling everyone what to do!"

"Jake is your leader," Jonah said mildly. "May I make a suggestion?"

"Of course," Jake said.

"Kesha said there's no reason to stay here. I agree."

"What do you think we should do?" Jake asked.

"You said there was evidence in Central Park, something that might explain what happened. Perhaps we should all go there."

Jake bowed his head in thought. Then, to Kesha's astonishment, he said, "Yeah, maybe you're right. Yeah, okay. We'll get everyone together and go up to Central Park tomorrow morning."

"What about David?" Cam asked. "He's waiting downstairs. What do you want me to tell him?"

Jake looked at Jonah. "Would you like to come with me? We could both talk to him."

Jonah nodded, and the two boys left the room.

Kesha was in a state of mild shock. "This is too weird. I've been bugging him forever. All Jonah does is open his mouth and Jake goes along with him."

"I can't believe he talked Jake into letting David back in," Martina grumbled. "But at least we're getting out of here."

"Yeah," Kesha said.

Martina looked at her. "Aren't you happy about that?"

"Sure." But Kesha had to wonder just who actually would be leading them. And where.

seven

donna stood in front of the health club and considered the weather. It could be so unpredictable at this time of year. Right now, at noon, it was almost warm, not hot, of course, but the sweatshirt she wore felt comfortable. She didn't need a jacket. But she knew it could get cooler later in the afternoon . . . still, if it didn't, did she really want to lug a jacket all the way uptown to Central Park?

She had to laugh at her ridiculous thoughts. If she needed a jacket at some point, she could pick one up easily enough. There was no shortage of stores uptown.

Martina came out of the club with a small pack on her back. "What's in there?" Donna asked her.

"Just the usual," Martina replied. "Underwear, toothpaste . . ."

"You don't have to carry that stuff with you," Donna pointed out. "There are plenty of stores around Central Park, you know."

"I know," Martina said. "But I wanted to have some basic things with me. Because who knows what's going to happen once we're there." She looked anxiously at Donna. "Sorry, I shouldn't be talking like that. I don't want to frighten anyone."

"I'm not frightened," Donna said. "It's funny, I thought I'd be scared to leave this area. But now that Jonah's with us, it's okay. I feel safe."

Safe, maybe. But not happy. She was having a hard time trying to stop her eyes from straying to the hotel across the street.

What was Travis doing, she wondered. Did he know that they were leaving the neighborhood? Was he looking out his window right that moment?

A hard knot started to form in her throat but she fought it back. She'd worked so hard these past few days at keeping her feelings under control, and she was getting better and better at it. She knew she wouldn't get any sympathy, not for a heartache, especially not when the heartache involved Travis. She could just imagine what Kesha's reaction would be.

Hanging around Jonah had helped. She couldn't say why, but his presence was comforting, and she found she didn't think about Travis so much. Still, every now and then, her eyes welled up and she had to look away, leave a room, do whatever she had to do so that no one would notice.

If they noticed . . . if Martina, or Jake, or any of them could see how she felt, they'd lecture her, they'd remind her that Travis had thrown her out, that Travis showed no concern for her welfare, and he wasn't worth crying over. They would point out that he couldn't love her if he treated her like that. And what could she say? Jonah's words came back to her. "Love is a feeling." That was the truth.

Over the past few moments, while she was in her reverie, all the rebels had gathered outside. Jake and Jonah were talking, probably about the route they'd take uptown. Alex and Shalini were huddled together, of course. Cam, Kesha, David and Adam all stood around, looking restless and ready to take off.

They gathered in a circle with Jake in the center. "I know we don't all walk at the same pace," he said, "but let's try to stay together, at least within a block. It might be a good idea for each person to have a partner, so that one person always knows where another person is. You don't have to stay together, just keep an eye on the person you're paired with."

Martina whispered in Donna's ear. "Wow, what a turnaround. He sounds so authoritative, like a real take-charge type. He's like a new person."

Jake was now assigning partners. "Okay." He looked over the group. "Alex and Shalini, Martina and Adam, Cam and Donna, Kesha and David, me and Jonah, okay? And I don't want to hear any complaints."

Kesha was standing nearby, and Donna could see that her ex-best friend wasn't particularly pleased with the arrangement. Donna wasn't surprised, though, when she didn't object. Kesha was smart, she had to know everyone was feeling pretty tense and that this was no time to make a fuss. Kesha was a very opinionated person, but she knew when to keep her opinions to herself. Kesha had a lot of superior qualities. Unfortunately, forgiveness wasn't one of them.

"We'll walk along Houston to Sixth Avenue," Jake continued. "Then stay on Sixth Avenue all the way up to Central Park."

"Why Sixth Avenue?" Martina asked. "Why not Fifth Avenue? The windows are better!"

Jake explained. "There are more grocery stores and delis on Sixth Avenue," he said.

"Has he been doing reconnaissance or something?" Kesha asked in a low voice.

"What does that mean?" Donna asked.

"Scouting."

At that very moment, they both realized they were speaking to each other, and edged apart. And Donna felt another pang, a different sort of pang, but just as strong as what she felt when she thought about Travis. She missed her best friend desperately, too.

The group began to move uptown, with Jake and Jonah in the lead. As they reached the end of the block, Donna turned back one last time to look at the hotel. She could have sworn she saw a curtain move in one of the windows. Was it Travis's window? Did it matter? Was this his last view of her?

Resolutely, she turned to face forward. She was in the approximate center of the group. Ahead of her, she saw that Jonah had dropped back from the lead. He was walking next to David, and David was talking to him. That was good, Donna thought. Jonah could be a good influence on David.

Martina was walking alongside her, and she echoed Donna's thoughts. "It looks like Jonah actually gets along with David. He must have the patience of a saint."

Donna agreed. "Jonah's amazing. I've never met anyone like him before in my life. He's pure kindness."

"Maybe that's because he has no memory," Martina said. "He has no history of bad feelings. I wonder what he was, before he got amnesia."

Donna considered that. "I'll bet he was a teacher."

"He's not like any teacher *I* ever had," Martina commented. "He doesn't order people around. But I can't picture him as some sort of businessman, either. Like you said, he's not like anybody. Look at the way everyone respects him."

"I don't think Kesha likes him," Donna said.

"Well . . ." Martina hesitated. "Kesha can be very stubborn."

Donna nodded sadly. "You don't have to tell me." She noticed that Cam had come up alongside her. "Cam, what do you think of Jonah?"

Cam said nothing.

"Cam?" Then she realized that Cam had a cassette player attached to his belt and a headset clamped to his ears. She poked his shoulder with her finger.

"Ow!" he yelped. But she'd caught his attention, and he took off the headset. "Yeah?"

"What do you think of Jonah?" Donna asked him.

He shrugged. "I don't know, I haven't thought about him."

Donna and Martina exchanged amused glances. That was typical Cam. He wouldn't know what was going on. As usual, he was lost in his own world.

"What music are you listening to?" Martina asked him, looking at the cassette player.

"I'm not listening to music," he said.

"What's on the tape?" Donna wanted to know.

He held the headset close to her ear so she could listen. She heard Cam's own voice, reciting a series of letters and numbers and symbols. "A-l-q-z, asterisk, semicolon, four, seven, g-r-u-e-p, three, exclamation point . . .''

"What is it?" Martina asked.

Donna handed the headset to her, and she listened for a moment. She looked just as confused as Martina. "Cam, have you completely lost your mind?" she asked pleasantly.

He wasn't offended. "I think it's a code," he told them. "I've been getting messages through the e-mail on my computer, and I recorded them on a cassette so I could listen to them while we walk. Maybe the key to the code will come to me."

Again, Martina and Donna exchanged looks, of disbelief this time. "You really think they're messages?" Donna asked. "From where?"

"I don't know," Cam said. "That's what I'm trying to find out." He clamped the headset back on, and retreated into his private, peculiar world.

Donna had estimated that the walk would take somewhere around two hours at a normal pace. But at the end of each block, Jake, or Jonah, or whoever was in the lead would wait for everyone to catch up. Since Alex and Shalini were always lagging way behind the others, that took a minute or two. After two hours, they'd only reached 34th Street, and people were getting hungry and cranky.

Jake led them into an Italian restaurant. "I think we should eat pasta," he declared. "We all need some complex carbohydrates, to improve our energy level and our mood."

"How does he know that?" Donna wondered aloud.

Kesha spoke to no one in general. "Now he's an authority on nutrition." But no one complained, and they all wolfed down the pasta and cheese.

Jake's newly discovered leadership qualities emerged again later when Shalini developed a blister on her foot. He saw the pain on her face, and he made them all wait while he went to the pharmacy. With a bandage and some cotton padding, Shalini was able to keep walking.

Along the way, Donna noticed that Jonah moved around a lot, talking—no, listening, actually. For a while, he walked with Alex and Shalini, and then Donna saw something truly amazing happen.

"Look at Alex!" she exclaimed. "He's smiling!"

"Ohmigod!" Martina and Kesha cried out in unison. They all cracked up. Then, just like before, Donna and Kesha realized they were communicating, sort of, and they both looked away.

"Oh, Kesha," Donna wailed, "don't be like this! Talk to me!"

Kesha's face went stony, she stared straight ahead and kept walking.

Donna didn't give up. "Look, I understand why you're angry at me. I should have talked to you before I ran off with Travis. But it was a last-minute decision, Kesha, and I couldn't help myself. I know you think he's scum, but I have feelings for him. I love him. And you're my best friend! That doesn't mean you have to love him too, but if you love me, you have to accept that I love him!"

She knew her voice had become very loud when she saw Alex and Shalini turn around and give her a look somewhere between shock and embarrassment. But she didn't care about them. She kept her eyes on Kesha. She thought she saw Kesha's lower lip tremble, and she could have sworn the glint of a tear was in her eyes. But even so, she wasn't surprised when Kesha quickened her pace and moved ahead rapidly. Kesha herself used to tell Donna that pride was her trademark. It was also her flaw.

As they neared Central Park, Jake stopped the group in front of a sporting goods store. "We need to pick up sleeping bags here," he called out.

"What do we need sleeping bags for?" Kesha asked. "There are plenty of hotels around Central Park."

Jonah spoke. "I agree with Jake. We should stay in Central Park."

"That's right," Jake said. "If we really believe something happened . . . something *landed* in Central Park, we should stay there, outdoors, if we want to make contact. Right?" He was looking at Jonah as he spoke, and Jonah nodded.

"Why do you need permission from *him*?" Kesha wanted to know. But it didn't matter, because everyone agreed.

They selected their sleeping bags from the large selection in the store. They stopped at a deli to pick up some easy-to-eat food—sacks of chips, cans of peanuts, stuff that didn't require cooking or utensils. They stopped at a newstand, to pick up magazines. There seemed to be an unspoken agreement among them—once inside the park, they wouldn't leave until something happened.

The group entered the park from 59th Street, or Central Park South, as this section of the street was known. Once inside, they followed the path that led past the playground and the Sheep Meadow, around the lake, and onto the Great Lawn. There, they settled, just on the perimeter of the vast, flattened circle of grass.

Donna paged through a magazine for a while, but soon the sun went down and there was no light to read by. She shared a bag of stale potato chips with Cam, and chatted with Jonah, mostly about how pretty the park was at night. Then he left her to talk with Alex and Shalini. Some of the group tired from the walk, immediately went to sleep. Donna kept reminding herself that she was surrounded by other people, and that there was no reason to feel as uneasy as she did.

She looked at where Martina had placed her sleeping bag, just a few feet away. Martina was sitting very still, her knees drawn up to her chest, her arms wrapped around her knees.

Donna went over to her. Martina didn't look nervous or frightened. In fact, there was a small smile on her face.

"What are you thinking about?" Donna asked her. "Your sister?"

Martina nodded. "I feel very close to Rosa here."

"Oh." Donna waited to see if Martina wanted to talk, but it was clear she wanted to be alone with her thoughts. So Donna went back to her own sleeping bag, and crawled inside. The air smelled sweet, and she felt herself dozing off right away.

When the elevator door opened on the penthouse level of the hotel, Ashley was greeted by the sight of two boys, Travis's buddies Ryan and James, huddled in front of a giant-screen TV. Both were so caught up in a Nintendo game that they didn't even notice Ashley. She had to stand in front of them and block their view of the TV to get any reaction.

"Hey!" Ryan cried in outrage. "Get out of the way!"

"I missed it!" James wailed. "It's your fault, Ashley!"

Ashley gazed at them both in extreme disdain. "Did you two revert to infancy or something?"

"Let's cancel the game and start over," James said to Ryan.

"Great," Ryan muttered. "And I was winning."

Ashley put her hands on her hips. "Hel-*lo*?"

"What do you want?" Ryan asked irritably.

"I want to see Travis," she said.

"He's busy," James said automatically. "Now get out of the way."

Ashley remained where she was. "You've been telling me that all day. I want to see Travis. Now."

"Look, he's busy, he's not seeing anyone today," Ryan yelled. "Are you going to move or do we have to move you?"

"What's he so busy doing?" she demanded to know.

"Who knows, who cares," Ryan muttered. Just then, the door to Travis's suite opened. Maura emerged.

"Maura," Ashley beseeched, "I have to see Travis, right away."

Now that Maura had taken on the role of the king's consort, she was suspicious of every other female in the community. "Why?" she asked suspiciously.

"It's important," Ashley said. She sighed. "Look, I don't have to see him alone, you can be there."

Maura still wasn't happy, but she seemed somewhat mollified. "Just a second," she said. She ducked back into the room, and reemerged a few seconds later. "Okay, come on in."

Ashley shot a look of triumph at Ryan and James, but they weren't paying attention. Great bodyguards, she thought.

Travis didn't appear to be particularly thrilled to see her either, but Ashley didn't let that bother her. She got right to the point. "Travis, I have to tell you about something," she began, but the sudden alarm on his face made her stop.

"Who left?" he wanted to know.

"Huh?"

"You're going to tell me someone else has left the Community, aren't you?"

"No, nothing like that."

He was relieved, but still not calm. "I keep waiting to find out who's going to desert us and betray me next. First Donna, then David . . ."

"Nobody's betraying you, Travis. David was only here for a couple of days. And Donna didn't desert you, you threw her out!"

"Personally, I'm glad David left," Maura said. "I think his mind's going. Travis, did you hear him telling that story about aliens landing in Central Park?"

He didn't seem to hear her. "I think he was a spy."

Ashley's brow wrinkled. "David Chu? A spy?"

"That's why he pretended to defect to us. He wanted to see what we have over here. You know, I saw him from the window this morning. They were all out front, together. I think they're forming an army."

"An army?" Ashley repeated. She looked at

Travis doubtfully, and wondered if someone else was losing his mind.

"What do you want?" he asked suddenly.

This was the hard part. Now *she* was about to sound like someone on the brink of insanity. But she plunged in. "I saw something on television. It was a person I used to know, and he was trying to speak."

Maura laughed. "You were just dreaming, Ashley. You told me yourself, you've been having weird dreams."

She shook her head. "Not this time, Maura. This wasn't a dream, I'm absolutely positive. Travis, something's out there, *people* are out there. Maybe Jake and the others are right. They're not dead, they're . . ."

"Where?" Travis challenged her.

"Out there," Ashley said lamely. "Look, all I know is that there's some kind of force that took everyone away, but they live, and they need us to save them."

Travis's face took on a patronizing expression. "Ashley, you were dreaming."

"No! Travis, please, you have to believe me, I wasn't dreaming!"

His expression went cold. "Then you're on the verge of a nervous breakdown. You'd better go to your room." He took her arm, politely but firmly, and put her out in the hall.

eight

at seven o'clock the next morning, Kesha was walking out of the Fifth Avenue hotel feeling a zillion times better. She was a city girl, not a camper type by nature, and she hadn't slept well in her sleeping bag on the hard ground. When she woke up, before everyone else, she felt grubby and achy. Then she remembered that the Plaza Hotel, one of the fanciest hotels in New York, was just south of the park, on Fifth Avenue. She took off in search of a shower.

She picked up a set of keys at random from the hotel reception desk. They unlocked the door to a room that had a super bathroom. The shower had six spouts that could shoot water at her from every angle with great force, and it felt like a massage on her aching bones. There was fancy soap and luxurious shampoo, and afterwards, she was able to wrap herself in super-thick towels. When she emerged from the hotel, she was a new person. And from the way she was greeted when she got back to the group on the Great Lawn, she decided she must look like a new person.

"Kesha!" Donna shrieked. "Look, Jake, there's Kesha!" They all came running toward her.

Kesha stepped back in alarm.

"Where are the others?" Jake demanded.

Kesha looked at them in utter bewilderment. "What others?"

"Cam and Martina!" Jake said. "They're missing too!"

"When we woke up this morning, you and Cam and Martina were gone," Donna told her.

"I wasn't missing," Kesha said. "I just went to take a shower, for crying out loud."

"Cam and Martina weren't with you?" Donna asked.

"No." By now, Jonah, Alex and David had joined them.

"Have you found them all?" David asked.

"Cam and Martina are still missing," Jake told him.

Serious concern crossed David's face. "What could have happened to them?" he asked worriedly.

Kesha looked at him skeptically. "What's the problem, you got the hots for Martina now?"

"We should set up a search party," Shalini suggested. "We could get some binoculars and go up to the top of the tallest building, see if we can spot them in the park."

"I hope they're together, at least, wherever they are," Alex murmured. "I hope they're not scared."

Kesha stared at him in disbelief. Since when did Alex start caring about anyone besides himself and Shalini?

"I think we should form search parties," Shalini stated.

"First of all, we have to stay calm," Jake declared. "We don't want to go running around in circles, we need to think this through rationally. Relax, everyone, we'll find them."

Suddenly, Donna let out a cry. "There's Cam!"

They all turned to look in the direction she was pointing. Sure enough, there was Cam, dragging a shopping cart loaded with boxes. As he drew closer, they could hear that he was whistling.

"Where have *you* been?" Donna wanted to know.

"Picking up stuff at Radio Shack," he told them. "I want to set up a remote control on-line system out here."

David let out a groan. "Don't go running off like that without telling people, okay?"

"Was Martina with you?" Alex asked anxiously.

Kesha felt like Alice after going through the Looking Glass. Everything was twisted. David and Alex were acting concerned, Shalini was speaking up and suggesting search parties—what was going on here? Did anyone else think this was a little weird?

She couldn't resist making eye contact with Donna. Donna looked straight at her, and made a face that clearly indicated she was also puzzled.

Cam didn't seem to be perturbed by anything. "I just saw Martina, back there," he said, cocking his thumb toward the path he'd come from. Then he began unloading boxes.

"Need some help?" Alex asked.

Cam paused, and studied him for a second. "Yeah, okay, you can help me open the boxes."

David and Shalini went to work on the boxes too. "I'll go get Martina," Donna said.

"I'll go with you," Kesha offered.

Donna gave her a little smile, and Kesha managed something like a smile too. They didn't say much on their way across the lawn, but it was a beginning. At least they were acknowledging each other's existence.

Martina was sitting on a bench, facing the path. "She looks strange," Kesha said in an undertone. "Is she okay?"

"I can't tell," Donna replied. "She's staring at something."

As it turned out, Martina was staring at nothing. Kesha crouched down in front of her. "Martina? Martina, are you okay?"

Martina gazed at her through glassy eyes, looking for all the world as if she was seeing a stranger. "Kesha?" she said wonderingly.

"What are you doing here?" Donna asked.

Slowly, Martina turned to face her. "Donna?"

Donna and Kesha exchanged anxious looks. "Maybe I should go get Jake," Donna said worriedly. "Or Jonah."

"What good could they do?" Kesha asked. "You might as well get David."

"David," Martina whispered.

"Oh, sorry, I forgot how much you hate David," Kesha said.

"I don't hate David," Martina murmured.

Donna blinked. "David? David Chu? Remember him? The creep who broke your sister's heart?"

"Oh." Martina's eyes were clearing. "Oh, right." She managed a half-smile. "I don't know what's the matter with me." She touched her forehead and winced.

"Does your head hurt?" Kesha asked.

"Yeah, a little."

"How did you get over here?" Donna asked again.

"I'm not sure . . . maybe I was sleep-walking." She touched her face again. "And, and maybe I fell." She stood up. Kesha and Donna each grabbed an arm to steady her.

"I'm okay," Martina said. She took a deep breath. "Yeah, I'm fine. Um, I think I'd like to be alone for a while."

"Okay," Donna said uncertainly. They left her there, but as they moved back toward the others, they both kept careful eyes on her.

"She says she feels fine," Kesha told Jake. "But I'm afraid she might have a concussion or something."

Jonah looked at her. "Why?"

"She's a little out of it. But everyone's acting kind of weird."

"What do you mean?" Jake asked.

"Well, look at Alex. He's acting like a person! Did you hear when he offered to go look for food? And he brought stuff back for everyone?"

"That was a kind thing to do," Jake said.

"Sure, it was kind, but it wasn't like Alex. And what about David? He's helping Cam hook up that computer stuff! Have you ever seen David help anyone do anything?"

Jake shrugged. He didn't appear too concerned. Jonah turned to Donna. "Do you think this is a problem?"

"I don't know if I'd call it a problem," Donna said. "But it's definitely strange."

"Maybe it's not really so shocking," Jake commented. "You know, situations like this can bring out the best in people. People start to bond in a crisis.''

"You might be right,'' Donna said. But Kesha couldn't buy that explanation. It seemed to her that they'd been in crisis since D-day, and no one had started bonding back then.

"What do you think, Jonah?'' Donna asked.

Kesha didn't particularly want to hear his opinion. "I think I'll go see how Cam's doing with his computer stuff.''

By the time she reached Cam, David had abandoned him. He was now teaching Shalini some sort of card game. Kesha looked around worriedly for Alex. But Alex seemed perfectly content, lounging under a tree and reading. He had to be able to see David hanging around Shalini, but he didn't seem to care.

Cam had set up his computer equipment right in the center of the flattened grass. He was in the process of attaching a high antenna. "How's it going?'' she asked.

"Fine,'' he said, without even looking at her. He sat down on the ground and turned on the power. A small light on the screen went on.

"It's working,'' Kesha noted.

"Of course it's working,'' he mumbled. "It's top of the line equipment.'' He hit some keys, and examined the screen. Then he stuck a disc into the disc drive.

"What's that?''

"Disc.''

"I *know* it's a disc. What's on it?''

"Messages.''

"What kind of messages?''

But now Cam had tuned her out. He was totally

concentrating on the gibberish that had appeared on his screen.

"Well, at least *you* haven't changed," Kesha commented.

There was no reply, but she didn't expect one. She left Cam and started away. Jonah and Donna were coming her way.

"How is Cam doing?" Donna asked.

"Okay," Kesha replied. "He's totally into that thing."

"Maybe I can help him," Jonah said suddenly.

"Do you know anything about computers?"

"I don't know," he said.

But Donna was intrigued. "Maybe you're feeling drawn to his computer for a reason. You could have been some kind of computer expert before you got amnesia."

"Cam doesn't want any help," Kesha said. "He likes to work alone."

"Can't hurt to offer," Donna said. She took Jonah's hand and they headed toward Cam. Kesha watched him and sighed. She hoped Donna wasn't developing a little crush on Jonah.

Ashley turned on her TV set. She'd been doing this every few minutes since she woke up that morning, but she'd seen nothing but the usual fuzz. She was starting to wonder if maybe seeing Corey actually had been a hallucination, like Travis thought. Or just a dream.

She'd certainly dreamed about him last night, and that dream had been more vivid than any of the others. This time, she knew he was calling for her to help him. She could even hear him. "Help me, Ashley, help me. I saved you, now you can save me.''

She owed him this. He was one of the most kind, decent people she'd ever known, and she wanted to save him. He saved her once, he cared about her, he kept her from becoming just another victim . . . And in the dream, she knew she could save him, she knew there was a way.

But when she woke up, she had no idea what to do next. How could she save him? She didn't know where Corey was, she didn't know where any of the missing people on earth were.

Travis wasn't going to help her, and if he wouldn't no one else here would either. She was on her own. She wished Jake was here . . . he would have believed her, he would have helped her figure out a way to reach Corey.

That wasn't the only reason she wished he was there. What was it that caused her to leave Jake a month ago? It seemed so unimportant now.

But Jake wasn't here. She was on her own. And she wasn't going to find Corey in this hotel room, that was for sure.

She had to get out of here. But where could she go? She kept the TV on, hoping Corey would reappear, tell her where he was and how she could get there. She paced the room. But nothing appeared on the TV, and nothing appeared in her mind either.

She rubbed her bare smooth head, as if the action could stimulate some new thoughts. She paused at her desk, where the hotel guest book was sitting. She'd never looked at it before—what was the point of examining a room service menu when you couldn't order room service? But it could be mildly amusing to see what they had to offer . . .

No, it wasn't amusing at all. Reading about stuffed chicken breasts and chocolate mousse only made her mouth water. Hastily she turned the page. The rest of the book consisted of ads for stores and Broadway shows. And there were the usual photos for tourists that showed New York at its best. Rockefeller Center at Christmas. Macy's Thanksgiving Day Parade. The Botanic Gardens in the spring, Central Park in autumn . . .

Central Park. What had she heard about Central Park recently? Oh yeah, last night, when she was arguing with Maura and Travis. Something about David and Central Park . . . suddenly, it was very important for her to remember exactly what Maura had said about David. Then it came to her, she could hear Maura's voice in her head.

". . . did you hear him telling that story about aliens landing in Central Park?" And Travis said something about seeing all the rebels being outside, in front of the health club yesterday . . . like an army, he said. Why like an army, she wondered? Were they marching? Marching uptown to Central Park?

The rooms across the hall faced the health club. She ran out of her room and banged on the door across from her. Andy Loomis answered the door wearing nothing but boxer shorts, and he ogled her. She realized she was still wearing a short nightgown, but she didn't care.

"I have to look out your window," she said and ran across his room.

"Why? What are you looking for?"

She peered over to the health club, wishing she had some binoculars as she looked for any movement inside.

"They're gone," he said.

She whirled around. "What?"

"I saw them, yesterday. They were all walking together."

"Which way?"

"Uptown."

Not bothering to reply, she ran out the door and back into her own room. Quickly, she went to the closet, and pulled out her clothes and sneakers. She dressed rapidly, wondering if she should look for a motorcycle or something to get her uptown faster.

She tore out of the room, and didn't even wait for the elevator. She went into the stairwell, and as she ran down the stairs, she tried to think of an excuse that would get the guard at the door to let her out without a buddy. Well, if she had to, she'd locate Maura and lure her out of the hotel with the promise of a makeover. And then, somehow, blow her off . . .

When she reached the bottom of the stairs, she paused to catch her breath and compose herself. Then she sauntered out into the lobby and went to the front door.

Mike Salicki immediately stepped in front of it, effectively blocking her from leaving.

"I need to go to a drugstore," she said.

"For what?" he wanted to know.

She pretended to be embarrassed. "Female stuff . . ."

He shook his head. "Write it down on this shopping list," he told her, indicating a notepad. "I'll be sending a couple of buddies out to get stuff later."

"But I need something *now*," she pleaded.

"Sorry," Mike said, though he didn't look sorry at all.

Ashley rolled her eyes. "Okay, I'll go find Maura so she can go with me."

To her surprise, Mike shook his head again. "That won't help. No one's going anywhere."

"Why not?"

"New rules."

"*What* new rules?"

"My new rules," came a voice from behind her. She turned to face Travis and Maura.

"Travis, what's going on?" she complained. "I need to get some stuff from a drugstore."

"Nobody's leaving this place," Travis said. "It's too dangerous."

"What are you *talking* about?" Ashley cried in frustration. She turned to Maura. "I was going to ask you if you wanted to come too. We could stop at that Swedish cosmetic store . . ."

Maura looked tempted but she shook her head regretfully. "We can't go, Ashley. Travis isn't letting anyone leave the hotel. He thinks the rebels are out there, hiding somewhere. He thinks they'll kidnap us."

"They've already kidnapped Donna and David," he said. "I'm not risking any more members of the Community."

"Travis! They weren't kidnapped!"

"I won't sacrifice my people," he insisted fiercely.

Ashley gaped. She looked at Maura. Couldn't she see that he was talking utter nonsense? But no, Maura liked being the leader's girlfriend. She wasn't going to contradict him.

Travis turned to Mike. "No one leaves."

Mike nodded.

There was nothing Ashley could do.

kesha moved around the flattened grass area, staring at the ground. Every now and then she gazed straight up into the sky. She had absolutely no idea what she was looking for in either direction.

She checked her watch, and at least there she found some useful information: it was four o'clock in the afternoon. They'd been here for . . . she couldn't remember what time they'd arrived at Central Park the day before, but she figured they'd been here almost twenty-four hours. Almost a full day. And what had happened? What were they doing? Nothing. Nothing at all.

But what *could* they be doing? Combing the grass for pieces of alien spaceship metal? Climbing trees to get closer to the sky and screaming up at something that might be hovering millions of miles above them?

If there *was* something up there, maybe they should be trying to attract attention. Maybe they should get some fireworks, the big spectacular kind, and set them off—would that make something happen?

"Hi, what are you doing?" Shalini stood there, smiling brightly at her.

"Nothing, really. Just thinking."

"What are you thinking about?"

Kesha looked at Shalini curiously. The Indian girl had never spoken to her in such a frank, friendly, open way before. She didn't think Shalini had ever spoken to anyone like this, except maybe Alex, and she'd never even heard her chatter brightly to him.

"Fireworks," Kesha told her.

"Fireworks?"

"Yeah. Big noisy ones, making colors all over the sky. I was wondering if that might help us to make contact."

Shalini smiled and nodded. "Okay. Let's get some fireworks."

"It's not that easy," Kesha pointed out.

"Why not?"

"Well . . ." She wondered just how naive Shalini could be. Did she actually think you could just walk into a store and buy spectacular fireworks? "They aren't exactly legal, for one thing. I wouldn't even know where to get them."

"Oh, that's too bad." Kesha realized that Shalini, *looked* different, too. The shiny black hair that was normally pulled tightly into a bun at the base of her neck was hanging wild and free. And her eyes weren't demurely lowered, either. They were bright, and wide.

Shalini pointed. "Kesha, did you see that big lake back there?"

"Sure, what about it?"

"There are boats tied up by that little building by the lake."

Kesha nodded. "Yeah, I know. That's the boathouse. You can rent rowboats there. Well, you *could* rent them. Now you can just take them.''

''And what do you do with them?''

How sheltered could Shalini be? ''Row them on the lake.''

''Have you ever done that?''

''No.''

''Do you want to go in a boat with me?'' Shalini asked eagerly.

Kesha hesitated. Shalini was giving her the creeps. ''Not really,'' Kesha said. ''Why don't you ask Alex to go in the boat with you?''

''Alex?''

''Your boyfriend, remember?''

Shalini brightened. ''You think he would?''

''Sure, he does everything with you, doesn't he?''

She smiled brightly again, and ran off in the direction of Alex—who was currently in the process of climbing a tree. Alex Popov, angry young man, sullen, pouting Alex Popov, who looked like he was born in a leather jacket, was scampering up a tree. And laughing.

What was going on here? Just a little while ago, she'd seen Donna trip on a rock, and David run over to help her up. And then she saw David talking to Martina—and Martina was actually talking to David. Everyone was behaving so peculiarly. Was it something they ate or drank?

Or maybe it had something to do with Jonah, she thought lazily. She still didn't trust him—he was too relaxed, too quiet. She wondered if Jonah could possibly have some sort of mysterious hypnotic skills that he was using on everyone . . . but why would he do something like that? And why was she immune?

She sat up suddenly. What if he was faking this amnesia business? What if he was just winning their trust so he could take over the rebel group? Of course, it made sense! That's why he stuck close to Jake, why he tried to spend some time with each rebel alone.

She had to talk to someone about this, to try out her theory. But who was left? She gazed around the outskirts of the Great Lawn. Cam was completely engrossed in his computer. David and Alex were in the tree, and she had no idea where Shalini had run off to. Jake was on the grass taking a nap! How could he sleep in the middle of the afternoon when they were supposed to be trying to contact aliens?

She didn't know where Donna was. And there wasn't anyone else. She counted rebels . . . she was leaving someone out. Oh, right, Adam. It was so easy to forget about Adam.

Then she spotted Martina, sitting under a tree. She went over to her, and sat down. "How are you feeling now?"

"Much better," Martina said. She put down her magazine.

"What are you reading?"

"Last month's *Seventeen*." She pointed to a photo. "Look, there's Ashley Silver."

"Oh yeah." Kesha examined the picture. "You like that skirt?"

"I wouldn't wear it," Martina said.

"Neither would I," Kesha agreed. At least Martina seemed to be acting normal. "Martina . . . have you noticed something strange?"

"Hm?"

"Some people are acting strange."

"Like who?"

"Shalini, for one . . . out of the blue, she's got this bubbly personality. Jake's acting like a wimp. Well, I guess that's not so strange, he was acting like a wimp back at the health club, moaning about Ashley. But I thought he got over that. I saw Alex laughing, can you believe that?"

Martina was listening with obvious interest, but she hadn't said a word.

"Haven't you noticed this?" Kesha asked.

"I'm not sure . . ."

"I saw you talking to David," Kesha went on. "Don't tell me you think he's behaving normally."

Martina gazed at her steadily. "No. David isn't behaving normally."

"See?" Kesha said triumphantly.

"Because he isn't David."

Kesha was sure she hadn't heard correctly. "What did you say?"

"He isn't David. I mean, he's David on the outside. But his brain . . . well, it's been borrowed. Sort of."

Kesha spoke uneasily. "Martina . . . are you sure you're okay?"

She nodded.

"What do you mean, his brain's been borrowed?"

"Well, not borrowed, exactly. Sort of possessed. Temporarily."

"By—by who?"

Martina shrugged. Her eyes went up. "I don't know. One of them."

Kesha could barely manage the next words. "One of them? Who are them?"

Martina pointed upward. "One of them that has the rest of us."

"How—how do you know this?"

Martina smiled, a little sadly. "Because I'm not Martina."

Kesha's breath came out in a rush. It was almost a full minute before she could take in enough air to speak. "Who are you?" she asked.

"Rosa."

For one wild moment, Kesha considered slapping Martina, with the hope that this might shock her back into reality. But as she looked into the other girl's eyes, she knew there was nothing she could do.

Because it was true. This wasn't Martina. This was her identical twin sister, Rosa.

"Where's Martina?" Kesha asked in a whisper.

"I'm not sure. Up there, I guess. Where I was."

"Where *were* you?"

Rosa made a gesture that clearly meant "Who knows?" "Wherever . . . wherever everyone is. Except for you guys, of course. You were all in Martina's geometry class, right?"

"Right."

"That's what I thought. I didn't know her schedule by heart, but I thought she had geometry fifth period. I was in western civilization."

"Rosa!" Kesha couldn't believe she was talking about Madison High School schedules. "Rosa, tell me what you know! Tell me what's happened!"

"Do you have any chocolate?" Rosa asked suddenly. "I'm dying for some chocolate."

"No. But we could go over to a store and get a bar."

"Could we do that now?" Rosa asked. "Because I'm not sure how long I'll be here.''

Kesha nodded. The two girls rose and started walking over to Fifth Avenue. Kesha was trying to formulate questions, and she didn't know where to begin. ''Where you are, I mean, where you've been, do you have food there?''

''We don't need food. We don't have bodies.''

''What are you?''

''It's hard to explain. It's sort of like we're nothing. Well, not nothing. We exist. I mean, we're aware, but there's no substance. It's like we're just spirits, or souls, or something like that.'' She spoke so calmly, so matter-of-factly, that Kesha found herself nodding, murmuring ''hm'' and ''yeah'' and acting like they were having a perfectly normal conversation. She tried to think of an intelligent question.

''Does it hurt?''

''We don't feel anything at all. I guess we're in suspended animation.''

Kesha shuddered. ''It sounds awful.''

''It's not, actually. Have you ever had nitrous oxide in a dentist's office? You know, the stuff they call laughing gas?''

''No.''

''Well it's kind of like that. We just sort of float.''

''And everyone's there? Every single person on earth?''

''I think so. It's not like we can actually see each other or anything like that. But it *feels* like everyone's there. You know what I mean?''

Kesha didn't have the slightest idea what she meant. ''Can you see . . . *them*? What do you call them, anyway?''

"I guess you could call them aliens. No, we can't see them. We *sense* them. That's how I know one of them is in David."

"Are they *bad*?"

Rosa shrugged. "We just know they're in control."

"What do they want?"

"I'm not sure," Rosa said. "They don't hurt us or anything. I think maybe they're studying us. Our brains, or souls, or whatever it is that we are."

"Why?"

"I don't know."

"Why didn't they take *us*?"

"I don't know."

They'd reached a small specialty food shop, and they went inside. "There's chocolate. It's probably a little stale, though."

Rosa peered into the glass case. "It's fancy stuff. I really just wanted something like a Hershey bar. Or M&Ms. Oh well." She went behind the counter and popped a chocolate into her mouth. "Mm. It's good. Want one?"

"No thanks. Rosa . . ."

"What?" She was putting chocolates into a paper sack.

"Do you know how you got back here?"

Rosa came out from behind the counter with her bag of candy. "Yeah. Well, I'm not positively *sure*. But it's got something to do with love."

"Love," Kesha said.

"Yeah. My sister cared about me so much, it's like she *loved* me back here."

"You mean . . . if we love someone enough, we can bring that someone back? No, that couldn't be it. I loved my mother, everyone here has people they loved."

"It's got something to do with our being identical twins," Rosa said. "But she couldn't just bring me back here. She could only trade places with me." They were back outside now. Rosa looked longingly down Fifth Avenue. "I don't think it's for very long, though."

Kesha looked at her in alarm, thinking Rosa might disappear at any moment. As they walked back into the Park, she began asking questions faster. "Can we get in touch with them? Can you get in touch with them for us? Can we talk to them?"

"Like I said, one of them is here," Rosa reminded her. "David's one of them. He's nobody important, though. And he won't talk to you about it. He wants to experience life as a person."

"Well, goody-goody for him," Kesha snapped. "Where's the real David?"

"Up there, with the others, I guess."

"Let's find the others," Kesha urged. "You can tell me if Shalini and Alex and the rest of them are real."

"I might not be able to tell you that," Rosa said. "I never really knew them. I knew David."

"Oh! That's right. You guys were together for a while, weren't you?"

"Yes." Suddenly, she stopped walking. She grabbed Kesha's arm.

"Are you okay?"

"Who's that man over there, talking to Cam Daley?"

"That's Jonah. He showed up last week. Donna found him wandering around on the Verrazano Narrows Bridge. He *says* he has amnesia. But I've got this feeling he's not what he says he is."

"You're right," Rosa said.

"What do you mean?"

"He's one of them."

"You mean, one of those aliens took over his body?"

"No, he's a *real* one, he's someone important."

"How can you tell?" Kesha asked excitedly.

"I don't know, I can, I can feel it!"

"Are we in danger?"

"I don't know," Rosa said again. "Kesha... I'm going to take a walk."

"I'll go with you," Kesha offered.

"No, if you don't mind, I feel like being on my own. I want to try to reach Martina." She said this as if she was going to the pay phone to call her sister. Kesha stared at her in bewilderment.

"I'll see you later," Rosa said, and she took off, heading back toward Fifth Avenue. Kesha just stood there, watching her go. Her head was spinning.

She wandered back toward the Great Lawn. She had to tell someone what she'd learned. Cam was alone now, playing with his computer. She hurried over to him.

"Cam, I have to talk to you," she said urgently.

He actually looked away from his computer and grinned. "Cool. I need a break."

"You do?"

"Yeah, I'm in a party mood. Hey, you know what we should do? Go back to Radio Shack, pick up a boom box, get some music, and dance!"

"Dance?" she asked faintly.

"Yeah, I feel like having some fun. Hey, Alex!"

She turned to see Alex coming toward them. His

smile was still startling to see. "What's up?"

"I think we need some music around here. Have a little party tonight, what do you think?"

"Sounds good to me," Alex said. "Where can we go?"

"There's a Radio Shack nearby," Cam said. He turned to Kesha. "You want to come to Radio Shack with us?"

Kesha shook her head. "No," she said. "I have to . . . find someone." Someone she could talk to, someone who was still a real person, a person she knew. Because Cam clearly wasn't.

ten

ashley lounged on a sofa in the hotel lobby and pretended to be studying an old copy of *Vogue*. Mike, still guarding the door, glanced in her direction every now and then. His eyes were narrow, and he seemed poised, ready for her to make a break for the door.

She didn't know what she was waiting for. Maybe Mike's shift at the door was almost over, and a more sympathetic guard would take his place.

She looked up when she heard the elevator doors open. Heather, Nicole, and Courtney came out chattering. They were all wearing jackets, and they looked like they were going somewhere. Now Ashley wished she'd been a little friendlier to them. She knew they thought she was a snob.

But maybe it wasn't too late. Just as they were about to pass her, she gave out a loud sniff. When that caught Heather's attention, Ashley wiped her eyes, as if she'd been crying. The girls looked at each other. Then Courtney shrugged, and all three approached Ashley.

"Are you okay?" Heather asked.

Ashley spoke in a choking voice. "I—I was looking at this magazine, and there's this article about new hair styles, and I started thinking . . .'' She let her voice trail off and touched her shiny head.

"Maura said you like it that way," Nicole declared. "She told me you shave it now."

"Well, I *had* to say that, didn't I? I don't want people feeling sorry for me."

The three companions seemed at a loss for anything to say. Finally, Nicole made an effort. "It'll grow back."

"But I want hair now," Ashley moaned. "I just can't stand looking like this any longer."

"You could get a wig," Heather suggested.

Ashley gasped, hoping her surprise seemed sincere. "Why didn't I think of that?" She rose from the sofa. "Would you guys come with me? There's a really nice wig store, up on 57th Street near the park."

Again the three girls exchanged looks. "Why do you want us to come with you?" Nicole asked.

"I need your opinion," Ashley said. "I can't make a big decision like this on my own. I want to try on a whole lot of wigs, and you guys could tell me which one looks best."

There was a spark of interest in Courtney's eyes. "You could pick up a whole bunch of wigs and have a different look for every day of the week."

"Hey, maybe we should all get wigs," Nicole said.

"Great idea," Ashley said enthusiastically. "Let's go."

She knew Mike would say they couldn't leave. And Mike was a pretty big guy. But there were four of them, and one of him, and she honestly believed he could be overpowered.

What she didn't take into account was the fact that her three new friends would be such wimps. "Oh, come on, Mike, please," Heather begged, and Nicole whined about not wanting to stay indoors on such a pretty day, but that was the extent of their efforts to escape.

"This is ridiculous," Ashley fumed. She spoke to the other girls. "We don't have to take this. He can't stop us from walking out."

"It's Travis's rule, not mine," Mike said.

"Why do you have to take orders from him?" Ashley challenged him. "You think he's better than you are?"

Uncertainty crossed Mike's face, and for a moment she felt a spark of hope. But then he crossed his arms across his chest. "I'm not taking orders from *you*, baldie."

Nicole gasped, and Ashley knew the girls were expecting her to burst into tears now. But from the way Mike looked now, she could tell it would be a waste of time. She stalked off to the elevator.

Back in her room, she tried to concentrate. There had to be a way she could get out of here. Ashley went to the window and looked down. She wasn't that high, this was only the third floor. If she opened the window and jumped, what would happen?

She would be toast. She could break both her legs. Even one broken leg would pretty much kill any possibility of getting up to Central Park. She looked around the room for an idea.

She recalled some stupid children's movie she'd seen once, where a kid ran away from home by tying sheets together and making a rope that he used to climb down from his window. She had sheets on her bed, and she knew where the linen closet was in the hallway . . . She looked back out the window.

It was too late for that. One of the buddies was standing guard by the side of the building. Travis might be losing his mind but he wasn't stupid. There were probably guards all around the building by now.

Could she gather all the others in the building, unite them to rise up against Travis and the buddies? No, she didn't have that kind of influence. Even if some of them were becoming dissatisfied with Travis's leadership, they weren't going to follow *her*.

They wouldn't even listen to her. They were all sheltered and fed. They felt safe. Their friends were here. Why would they want to leave? For what? Freedom? What could that word mean anymore in a world without possibilities?

But there *were* possibilities, she knew that now. The twenty-five seniors from Madison High might be the last people on earth, but they weren't the only people in the universe. Corey had essentially told her that. He wasn't the type to beg for help for himself alone. Others . . . maybe *all* the others were with him, somewhere.

Only she wouldn't be able to convince the Community of that. They'd believe what Travis and Maura believed, that she was having a nervous breakdown or something like that. The people who would have listened to her—Jake, Martina, Donna, Cam, Kesha—they weren't here. It wasn't as if she had any friends here, people who really knew her and trusted her. She'd never allowed that to happen. She was paying for it now.

She was trapped. Trapped like a caged animal in a burning building. There was no way out.

A burning building, flames leaping into the air . . . why had that image appeared in her mind? Fire . . .

She went to her door. *In Case of Fire* was the first line of the notice hanging there. The second line read *Know Your Exits*. She studied the map. She closed her eyes and tried to take a mental photograph of it.

She put her hand on the doorknob. Tentatively, holding her breath, she turned it, praying there wouldn't be a buddy right out there on her hall. Slowly, she opened the door a crack and peered out. The hall was empty.

On tiptoes, she ran to the end of the hall. The door marked FIRE EXIT was right where the map told her it would be. With all her might, she pushed on the steel bar.

The alarm came, fast and furious. She'd never heard such a loud fire alarm in her life. She flew down the stairs. Through the thick walls, she thought she heard some cries of panic. She'd just reached the bottom level when the fire door on that landing opened. One of the buddies stood there.

Before he could speak, Ashley screamed out, "Fire, fire! Get out!"

The boy turned white. He pushed Ashley out of the way. She followed him down a few more stairs, and then out another door.

She was outside now. It looked like half the Community was already out there. People were running around, looking frightened, yelling, "Where's the fire? Where's the fire?"

Ashley didn't linger to find out.

Kesha was in the boathouse. It wasn't a particularly comfortable hideout, but it would do for the moment, while she gathered her thoughts and tried to decide what to do. From the windows, she could see some of her fellow rebels. There were boys in the trees . . .

A window on the other side looked out on the lake. She could make out Shalini and Donna in a rowboat, floating in the middle.

Cam was gone now, that was clear. He'd left to get a boom box, but that wasn't all. A party alien had taken over his mind. Shalini was gone, David, Alex, probably Jake. So who was left besides her? Adam Wise . . . but she couldn't be certain of that. How would she know if Adam was behaving normally or not? He was pretty much a cipher. She didn't think anyone there really knew him.

Rosa had said the possession was temporary. But what did that mean? Would they be possessed for an hour, a week? A year? And how could Rosa be sure of that anyway?

Unless Rosa was one of them too. Rosa might not be Rosa, she could be an alien inside Martina. No, she couldn't believe that. She'd known Rosa, before, and that *was* Rosa she'd been talking to. But she had no idea where Rosa was now.

Donna . . . was Donna still Donna? And why had nobody taken over *her*, Kesha? Why did her mind still feel perfectly intact? Because she was the only black person here? Were the aliens racist?

She went back to the window. Donna and Shalini were still on the lake. From this distance, she couldn't tell if they were talking. Surely, if Donna was still Donna, she'd know by now that Shalini wasn't Shalini.

She couldn't just stand here, she had to do something.

She dragged a rowboat out to the lake. She'd never done this before in her life, but how hard could it be? She'd seen people rowing in the lake here before. If she could just manage to keep from throwing up, she'd be okay.

She got into the boat, and held her breath while it bobbed in the water. She wasn't nauseous, that was good. Unfortunately, the boat had already drifted away from shore before she remembered that they usually had oars with them, to make the boat move.

She tried using her hands, flapping them back and forth in the water, but it was useless, the boat was going to go wherever it went. It wasn't going anywhere near Donna and Shalini.

She pulled off her hiking boots, and her socks. She stripped down to her underwear. Then she dove into the lake.

It was cold, and she knew it had to be pretty filthy, but she tried to block that from her mind. It wasn't easy, especially when an empty soda can bobbed in front of her eyes. But she gritted her teeth, and swam.

Shalini—pseudo-Shalini, actually—saw her first. She waved gaily. "Hi! Is that fun?"

"No," Kesha sputtered. She grabbed onto the side of the rowboat. "I mean, yes! Yes, it's great fun, you should try it!"

"Okay," Shalini said. Ten seconds later, she was in the water. "Oh, this doesn't feel so nice."

But Kesha wasn't paying any attention to her

now. She'd clambered into the boat and she was facing Donna. "Donna, Donna, are you there? Is that you?"

Donna's face was expressionless. She wasn't reacting to Kesha's appearance at all.

"Donna!"

Still, nothing, no response. This wasn't how the other possessed kids were acting. But it wasn't like Donna either. Was she in the process right now? What should she do?

Rosa's words came back to her. "My sister cared about me so much, it's like she loved me back here."

Donna wasn't her twin. But she was her best friend, and that had to count for something. And if she was just in the process of transition . . .

"Donna, listen to me!" There was no indication whether Donna heard her, but she kept talking. "I was stupid, I had too much pride, you were always telling me that was going to get me into trouble. And it did, because I couldn't forgive you when you ran off with Travis. Only I *wanted* to forgive you. Deep in my heart, I couldn't hate you, not then, not ever. You're my best friend, Donna, my very best friend in all the world, and best friends never stop loving each other, no matter what. Don't leave me, Donna, I need you!"

Donna spoke slowly. "What are you talking about?" Her voice was thick, she sounded almost drunk.

Kesha spoke rapidly, saying everything that came into her head. "There's no one I can talk to like I talk to you; there's no one who cares about me as much as you do! And I care about you more than anyone else around here, I know all your secrets, about your nasty father and your alcoholic mother—you've told me things you've never told anyone else, I've told you secrets too, and you know how I hate to tell personal secrets . . .'' She was rambling now, talking without thinking.

But the emotions were there, and they were true. She might not be expressing her feelings very well, she knew she was coming on too strong, but she also knew that the basic feelings were honest, they were deep and real, she could feel the power of those feelings . . .

And so could Donna. The fog over her eyes lifted. For a moment, she looked puzzled. ''What are we doing out here on the lake?''

''It's a long story,'' Kesha said. She grabbed an oar that lay on the bottom of the boat and began to paddle to shore.

Donna rubbed her forehead. ''I have the weirdest headache. Like something's trying to get inside my head.''

''Alien possession,'' Kesha said.

''What?''

''I'll explain later.'' They'd reached the edge of the lake, and Kesha jumped out of the boat.

Shalini was there, sitting on the bank, her feet in the water. ''I'll stay here for a while,'' she called out as Kesha and Donna dragged the boat out of the water. ''Then we can go in again.''

''Yeah, whatever,'' Kesha said. Shalini seemed like a nice girl, but Kesha couldn't say she loved her. There was no way she'd be able to help Shalini lose her possession.

She grabbed Donna's hand. ''Come on!''

''What's going on?'' Donna asked in bewilderment. And then, "Oh, Kesha, look! There's Ashley!"

"What?!"

Sure enough, standing alone at the rim of the crushed grass on the Great Lawn was Ashley Silver. Relief washed over her face when she saw Kesha and Donna approach.

"Where is everybody?" she asked, and at the same time, Kesha asked, "What are you doing here?" Then Ashley said, "I escaped from the Community," while Kesha said, "Aliens borrowed their brains."

Donna's head turned back and forth between them. "Uh, Kesha, I think you'd better talk first."

Kesha took a deep breath. "They're not dead. The others. They're being held. And the ones who are holding them, they're getting into our heads."

She told them about Rosa, and the possessions, and who Jonah was, and the existence of the rest of the world. As the words poured out, they sounded like utter insanity to her own ears. But the passion was there, and so the bizarre words came across as truth.

"Jake," Ashley murmured. "What happened to Jake?"

"I'm not sure," Kesha said. "But he was spending an awful lot of time with Jonah. The last time I saw him he was taking a nap on a slope over there." She led Donna and Kesha in that direction.

Jake was still there, still asleep. "Is it him?" Ashley wondered. "Or one of them?"

"Rosa said love is the key," Kesha murmured.

Ashley fell down beside the sleeping Jake. She began to whisper into his ear. Jake stirred. His eyes opened slightly. His lips moved as if he was trying to speak but no sound came out. Ashley touched his cheek and spoke softly. He said something the others couldn't hear. And even though they were both fully clothed, and they weren't touching, there was something so intimate, so very, very personal and private about the moment that Kesha had to turn away, and so did Donna.

Kesha saw Donna's eyes get misty. "Don't tell me you're thinking about Travis," she groaned.

"I can't help it," Donna said simply.

Kesha relented. She put an arm around her best friend's shoulder and gave her a little hug. "Yeah, okay. I'll deal with it."

There was a rustling behind them, and they turned back to the couple on the grass. Jake was trying to sit up. Ashley had both of her hands on his shoulders. She pushed him back down and planted a long, hard kiss on his lips.

Gently, Ashley released him. He lay there, staring up at her. Then he smiled. "You came back," he said.

She leaned over, gave him another kiss, and said, "So did you."

He sat up. "What's going on? Where are the others?"

A voice behind Kesha said, "They're gone."

Kesha turned around and faced Alex. "What do you mean, they're gone?"

"What was in my head," Alex said.

"Yeah, me too," David echoed. He looked dazed. "Me, and Alex, and Adam, we were climbing this humungous tree, and then suddenly, it was just me and Alex." He frowned. "What the hell was I doing in a tree?"

"Where's Adam?" Jake asked. They all began

looking around. Shalini was no longer on the banks of the lake. They didn't see Jonah, or Cam.

But they found Rosa, sitting on the park bench. Jake hurried over to her. "Martina, have you seen Cam or anyone else?"

"That's not Martina," Kesha declared. She had to admit to a certain pleasure in knowing stuff Jake didn't know yet. "It's Rosa. They changed places."

Jake looked at Kesha as if she'd gone crazy.

"It's true," Kesha insisted. "Tell him, Rosa."

She shook her head. "I'm not Rosa. I'm Martina."

Jake smirked at Kesha. "I think you need to get your head examined."

"I was released," Martina continued. "Rosa's gone back. With Jonah."

Now Jake was staring at Martina in horror. "Jonah?"

"Did he force her?" Kesha asked.

"She did it so I could come back."

"What are you talking about? Come back from where?

"Didn't you feel it, Jake?" Martina asked. "Didn't you feel something coming into your mind?"

Realization flooded Jake's face. He was clearly stunned—but Kesha could see that he believed what he was learning.

"Where's Cam?" Kesha asked. "And Shalini?"

"I'm here," a small voice responded.

Shalini had crept up behind them. She huddled next to Alex, and he promptly put a comforting arm around her. Her voice and manner told Kesha that she'd been released too.

"It was the weirdest feeling," David said. "Like someone was visiting in my head. Borrowing me. But I was still here too. And I wasn't scared."

"Is that how it was for you?" Ashley asked Jake. "Was someone inside your head?"

"No . . . I just felt like someone was *trying* to get in."

Kesha grinned at him. "Ashley saved you."

"How?"

Martina explained. "I *think*, if someone loves you enough, they can't get into your head."

Donna looked at Kesha, and Kesha's grin turned into an embarrassed smile. "I don't think it has to be *romantic* love."

"There's Cam now," Martina declared.

He was coming along the path that led from the West Side, with another Radio Shack box in his arms. He looked excited.

"I think I've got it!" he crowed.

"You've got what?" Jake asked.

"The key to the code! I don't think it was a code at all, I think the messages were created through another processing program, one that my computer couldn't format to read. That's why it looked like gibberish on the screen. So I got some software, and I should be able to convert the files with it." He ran off to the Great Lawn, where his computer equipment was set up.

"Well, Cam is Cam again," Kesha said. Then she frowned. "But I don't get it. If love is the key to getting real, how did Cam lose his visitor, or whatever it is that got into his head? I mean, Cam's a good guy, and we all like him, but who loved him enough?"

"I don't know," Martina said. "Maybe love for your work counts too."

Jake was getting excited. "Then we can bring everyone we love back?"

"No," Martina said. "It's not that easy. There's something more to it, but I don't know what it is. Love is the key. But it's not enough. I only know what Rosa's communicated to me. And she doesn't understand it all yet."

"Where's Adam?" Jake asked suddenly.

"I think he's with Rosa and Jonah," Martina said.

Jake was distressed. "Why?"

"Did you really know him all that well?" Martina asked him.

"No, not personally."

Martina gazed at the others. "Did any of you know him well?"

No one spoke.

"That's it, then," Martina said sadly. "There wasn't enough feeling to keep him here."

Kesha sat down on the bench next to Martina and spoke in a whisper. "Then what about David? Why is *he* still here? Nobody loves him."

Martina grimaced. "My sister still does."

"Oh."

"Martina . . ." Ashley asked hesitantly. "What was it like . . . there?"

"It's hard to say. Not good, not bad." Martina contemplated the question. "Have you ever had nitrous oxide in a dentist's office?"

"I've got it! I've got it!" Cam was yelling at the top of his lungs as he ran down the slope toward them. "The e-mail messages, I know what they say!"

The light of discovery made his eyes shine. "There's another group like us, kids who weren't taken. They're out in California, in Los Angeles. They've been sending out random messages, that's what I picked up!"

"You mean, it really was a code?" Kesha asked.

"No, it wasn't a code. The software I had couldn't read their messages, that's why they came out like gibberish!"

"Who are they?" Donna asked.

"I'm not sure. They say they're a group of teens, I don't know how many. But it looks like they've been through the same experience. Everyone disappeared, except them. They've been sending out messages at random, just like I've been doing, trying to find if there's anyone else."

"Do they know we're here?" Jake asked.

"I executed an 'answer sender' message, I don't know if it will work. We have to get out there, we have to join forces with them!"

Kesha turned to Martina. "I guess you're right. Love for work must count too."

"What are you talking about?" Cam asked her.

"Why you're still here. Whatever possessed your mind wasn't as strong as your love."

Cam appeared mildly insulted. "Nothing was possessing my mind."

Kesha rolled her eyes. "Cam, I saw you, I talked to you. You wanted to have a dance party. You weren't Cam."

He grinned. "I was just faking it. So I'd have an excuse to go to Radio Shack and Jonah wouldn't try to stop me." He turned back to Jake. "I'm serious about going to California. That's what the message was saying. It was telling everyone who could read it to get to Los Angeles. I even have an address.''

''Great,'' Jake groaned. ''How are we going to get to Los Angeles? Walk? Drive? The way the roads are cluttered, it would take almost as long as walking.''

''Fly.''

It was Donna who said this. They all looked at her.

''You plan on growing wings?'' Kesha asked lightly.

''Travis has a pilot's license.''

eleven

Cam was busily transferring all the information from the e-mail messages onto discs. He was trying to work fast before the sky went completely dark. "It's a shame to leave all this fabulous equipment here," he said sadly. "One good rain, and it will be toast."

"Tough," David said without pity. "I'm sure there's plenty of junk like that in California. Silicon Valley, remember?" He rubbed his hands together in glee. "Oh, man, I could do with a day at the beach. Don't forget your bikinis, girls."

Martina gazed at him with unconcealed dislike. "I'll never understand Rosa," she said to Donna. "Abducted by aliens, and she's still hot for that jerk."

"Love defies explanation," Donna murmured.

Kesha looked at her meaningfully. "You should know." Then she put up her hands in mock defense. "Okay, okay, just kidding."

"The important question," Cam said, "is how are we going to get Travis to fly us to California?"

"We're going to show him what you've got on those discs," Jake said. "Travis isn't stupid. He'll see that he has to go along with this."

"I don't know why you think he'll understand," Martina said. "He doesn't want to accept that there's anyone or anything out there. Even before, when we showed him the evidence, he totally ignored it."

"This is different," Jake said stubbornly. "He'll listen this time." But he sounded like he was trying to convince himself.

"Don't count on that," Ashley warned. "He's getting weirder."

Jake's voice hardened. "Then we'll have to force him."

"How?" Cam asked.

"You're the brainiac," Jake shot back. "You come up with an idea."

Cam placed the loaded discs into his jacket pocket and considered this. "Kidnap him at gunpoint?"

"Gee, I really needed a genius mind to come up with that suggestion," Jake said sarcastically.

"Come on, guys, let's get going," Kesha urged. "Maybe we'll come up with an idea along the way."

They stopped at a store to stock up on chocolate bars for quick energy. Then they started downtown.

"So, let me get this straight," David said to Martina as they were walking. "That wasn't just Rosa's mind in your body. That was really Rosa."

"Yes," Martina said.

"In her own great body."

Martina scowled at him.

"Hey, don't look at me like that!" David yelped. "I didn't come on to her. It wasn't even me!"

Donna turned to him in interest. "What did it

feel like for you? When you were, you know, not in your body?"

"I just felt like I was floating above it all," David said. "I could see me, but I wasn't part of me. It was sort of like the time I dropped acid . . ."

"Please don't share that experience with us," Martina said. To the others, she said, "There's still a lot I don't understand. The aliens who were in Alex and David—they weren't hostile. In fact, in some cases they were an improvement." She shot David a look. "And how come Jonah was here in person? Why did he have a real human body?"

"Maybe he's their leader," Jake said. "But you know, he wasn't hostile either. I mean, I never felt threatened by him, did you?"

"Not really," Kesha admitted. "I thought there was something weird about him. But he wasn't frightening."

"And why were some minds occupied and not others?" Martina continued. "Kesha, you never felt anything, did you?"

Jake laughed. "Kesha scared them away. Look, what I can't figure out is why they just didn't zap us off the earth, like they did to everyone else."

"Maybe when we meet the California group, we'll find a common denominator," Cam said.

"Hey, you know what?" David said. "That guy inside me . . . he was having a good time, I could feel it." He said this proudly, as if his body had been a better place to occupy than any of the other bodies.

"He was probably absorbing the alcoholic remnants of your last party," Jake noted.

They were walking a lot faster this time than when they walked uptown, so they reached Soho in less than two hours. As soon as they crossed Houston Street, Jake stopped them.

"Now, I don't know what we're going to find when we get to the hotel," he said. "But we have to be prepared for anything. Ashley told you what was going on when she escaped this afternoon. They must know she's gone by now, so some of them may be out looking for her. Or, they could all be inside the hotel."

"Travis was becoming totally paranoid," Ashley continued. To Donna, she added, "I'm sorry, but it's true."

Donna just nodded. She wasn't doubting what Ashley said. She was trying to figure out how to deal with the paranoia.

"They could be armed," Ashley went on. "Some of the buddies have been wanting to do that for a while."

"Travis doesn't like weapons," Donna said.

Ashley spoke to her kindly. "But Travis isn't behaving rationally, Donna. Or maybe the other guys have mutinied. We don't know."

"How should we approach them?" Cam asked.

"I'll go in," Jake said. "Alone. I'll tell Travis we want to surrender and rejoin the Community. I'll tell him we want to have an official ceremony of surrender to turn over the flag."

"What flag?" Kesha asked.

Jake thought. He looked around the gutter, and picked up a bent wire coat hanger. Then he took off his shirt, and pulled his undershirt over his head. He straightened out the hanger, and tied the arms of the undershirt around it. He presented it to Kesha.

"I'm carrying the flag?" she asked.

"Yeah. I need someone who can look proud."

Kesha grinned. "That's me."

They fell silent, and they found themselves almost marching in procession as they headed to the hotel. Kesha, walking alongside Jake, held the undershirt flag up. Behind them were Martina and Cam, side by side, and bringing up the rear were Donna and David.

They could hear noise coming from the hotel before they could even see it, and they stopped before they rounded the corner.

"What is that?" Ashley asked.

David frowned. "Acid jazz. Man, I hate that stuff. You can't dance to it."

"It doesn't sound like they're preparing for war," Martina told Jake. Even so, Jake led them through an alley so they could approach the hotel from the back. They crouched down by the plastic recycling cans.

"Okay, everyone stay here," Jake whispered. "I'm going in."

"No," Donna said. "*I'm* going in." And before anyone could react or stop her, she ran from them and around to the front door.

She'd started planning this just a short while back, when Ashley had said that Travis wasn't behaving rationally. Rational, logical, those were Travis's middle names. Ashley couldn't know that. But Donna did.

Ashley had chalked his behavior up to the onset of paranoia. Donna was thinking it could be something else, something only she could resolve. She pushed open the door.

Mike, Travis's right-hand man, along with Ryan

and James were standing there. All three were taken by surprise.

"What are you doing here?" Mike demanded to know. "You were banished from the Community."

She bowed her head. "I want to see Travis."

"Forget it."

"I have to talk to him," she said.

"No way. Get out of here." Mike grabbed her roughly by the arm. And at that moment, Donna utilized her secret weapon. She started to cry.

It wasn't much of a talent, this ability to produce tears at will. But it had gotten her out of trouble a few times at home, and she'd managed to avoid a suspension for cutting class one day by crying in the principal's office. She knew it would come in handy again.

And she knew something else. Nothing in the world could make a boy feel more uncomfortable than to see a girl cry. Boys could deal with anger, or pouting, or just about any other show of emotion. But not tears.

She cried hard and noisily, and she could feel Mike's grip on her arm relaxing. "Hey, cut that out," he said gruffly.

She had to close her eyes to make the tears happen, but she opened them a crack to judge the reactions of the other two boys. Every bit of macho self-confidence had evaporated from the faces of Ryan and James. Ryan was studying the ceiling, James was intensely examining the floor.

She raised her tear-stained face to Mike, whose face reflected a combination of embarrassment and disgust and a general desire to die right then and there. "Please," she whimpered. "Please."

He let go of her arm. "Just get out of here," he

mumbled. But he wasn't pushing her out the door. She sniffled loudly.

"Get out!" he begged.

At that moment, she heard the elevator doors open, and she took off. She was forced to practically shove poor Nicole out of the way so she could get on the elevator and hit the CLOSE button before Mike and the others could react.

"Don't stop, don't stop," she pleaded silently as the elevator made its way up to the penthouse. It didn't.

She stepped back into the shadows cautiously as the doors opened on the top floor. She knew Scott and Kyle would be guarding Travis's door.

Praise Nintendo. If she had the time, she would have dropped to her knees and offered thanks to the giant screen and its cartoon monsters.

"Shoot him, shoot him!" Kyle was yelling to Scott. "You stupid idiot, give me that!"

While he was wrestling the controls from Scott, Donna made a mad dash from the elevator to Travis's door.

Travis and Maura were sitting on the sofa, watching a video. They both jumped up when they saw Donna.

Donna looked at the screen. Julia Roberts and Richard Gere. She practically choked. Travis hated romantic comedies. His mind couldn't be in his own control.

"Get out of here!" Maura shrieked. "Kyle! Scott! Help!"

But even Maura's shrill voice couldn't drown out the sound effects of Nintendo. Donna ignored her and went directly to Travis. Her unexpected shove sent him back down into a sitting position on the sofa, and she jumped on his lap to keep him from getting up.

"I love you," she said fiercely. "I love you!"

She could feel Maura's long sharp nails digging into her shoulders, but she kept her concentration on Travis's stunned face.

"She doesn't love you, she just wants power and prestige. You knew how I felt about you, how I still feel. Even if you had lost the student council election, I would have stayed with you. I love you more than anyone else in the world could ever love you. You're an egomaniac, you're a snob, you're conceited and selfish and self-centered and totally unworthy of my love, but I love you anyway, I can't help it! Travis! Do you hear me?"

He stared at her. "Have you lost your mind?"

"No, it's your mind! Something's in there!"

Travis actually looked nervous. "Maura . . ."

"I'll get help," Maura said. She ran out of the room. Donna jumped off Travis's lap and ran after her. As soon as Maura was out the door, Donna locked it.

"What do you think you're doing?" Travis bellowed.

"You're not yourself, Travis!"

"I'm not? Who am I?"

His eyes were clear. And Donna knew she'd made a mistake. She swallowed with difficulty. "Why were you watching that movie?"

"I wasn't," he said. "I was taking a nap. Maura must have stuck it in the VCR. She's got terrible taste in movies. What are you doing here? If you think we're going to take you back, you better think again."

Now there was a pounding on the door, and

shouts of "Open up or we'll break it down!" Donna knew she didn't have much time.

"Travis, listen to me. Remember Jonah?" She spoke as quickly as she could, and just hoped she was making sense. "You were right about him. He wasn't what I thought he was."

The words spilled out of her. At any moment, she expected Travis to shove her aside and open the door to his guards. Or just throw her out. He could do it, he was much stronger than she was.

The door was making ominous noises. It wasn't going to hold forever. She had to think fast.

"We need you, Travis," she said. "It's not just me, it's all the rebels. We're desperate. We have to fly to California, and you're the only one who can take us there."

He started toward her. She held her ground and kept talking. "There are others out there, Travis. Other survivors. Cam made contact with them. We have to meet them. The people who are gone, they still exist; we might be able to get them back here."

He pushed her aside. He was moving past her now, toward the door. She did the only thing she could think of doing—she ran behind him and jumped up onto his back.

"Get off me!" Travis yelled.

She heard the door begin to crack. "Travis, we need you!" There was a moment of hesitation in his efforts to throw her off his back, and then she knew the magic words. "You could take over! You could be our leader! Those people in California, there could be lots of them, they'll need you too. Jake's a wuss, you know that, he can't handle a big group. You could lead the mission to get everyone back, you'll be a hero, you'll rule the world!''

The door shattered. Scott, Kyle, Maura, and three others were standing there, gaping at the sight of Travis with Donna clinging to his back like a child getting a piggyback ride.

"There's a bunch of rebels outside," Scott reported. "Want to come with us? We're going to trash them."

"I'll talk to them," Travis said. "Donna, get off my back."

She did. Everyone crowded onto the elevator and went down to the lobby. Through the glass doors, she could see Kesha holding the white flag. "See?" she said to Travis. "They don't want to fight."

"We're coming too," Mike said.

"No," Travis said. "Wait here."

"Aw, come on," one of the guys begged. "We want to kick some rebel butt."

"Not yet," Travis said, and he went outside with Donna. He stood face to face with the rebels. Before anyone could say anything, Donna spoke. "I told Travis he would be our new leader."

Jake's face darkened, and Kesha looked like she was about to choke or explode.

"Is this true?" Travis asked. "Donna says you're desperate, you need real leadership." He was looking directly into Jake's eyes. "She says you can't handle this."

Oh, Jake, don't be proud, Donna begged silently. It's the only way we'll get him to come with us. And Kesha, you're my best friend, but please, please, please, keep your big mouth shut for once.

She'd never really believed in telepathic communication, but maybe there was something to it.

In any case, Kesha didn't speak. And Jake nodded. Fortunately, Travis couldn't see the struggle going on in his eyes as he spoke.

"Yeah. We need you to take over."

Travis nodded. "Let's go to the airport."

Behind them, the door to the hotel opened. "Hey, what's going on?" Mike yelled. "Travis, you need help?"

"Stay back," Travis called.

But they weren't taking orders anymore. "Let's get 'em," someone screeched. The rebels took off.

They had a good head start on the Community people who were coming after them. Donna gripped Travis's hand as they ran behind the others. Jake was in the lead, but she had no idea where he was taking them. They turned a corner, and when Donna and Travis caught up, they'd all disappeared. Then she realized they must have gone down into a subway entrance.

"Come on," she urged Travis.

"Into the subway?" he asked. It dawned on her that this was probably the first time in his life that the upper-class Travis Darrow had ever considered entering a subway station.

"Sorry, no limos are available," she said. "Come *on*!" She could hear the Community members getting closer. For once, Travis obeyed.

At the bottom of the stairs, tall metal gates barred their way. "Great, we're trapped!" Travis sneered. "Good work, Robbins."

But Jake had not washed his jeans for some time. From his pocket, he withdrew a Metrocard. He stuck it in the slot, and it released the gate for one person to pass through. Then he pulled the card back out, and each of them used it to get in.

The others were close behind them. As the group went down the stairs into the subway tunnel, they could hear the Community guys yelling and banging on the gates that barred their way.

But apparently none of them had a Metrocard, and there was no way they could break down those gates. New York City Metro Transit didn't make it easy for fare jumpers.

twelve

none of them felt too terrific when they came to the area of Brooklyn known as Howard Beach—a strange name, Ashley thought, since she certainly didn't see any signs of a beach around there. They'd been walking for a long time, maybe four hours, closer to five, two of them in the filthy underground. Fortunately, the disappearance of all life-forms included rats.

It was still dark out. Travis looked at the sky worriedly. "I've never flown at night," he said.

Jake looked at his watch. "Don't worry, it will be dawn by the time we get to the airport. We still have a walk ahead of us."

He was clearly exhausted, just as all of them were, but somehow he managed to keep his voice calm, steady, and confident without coming across as too authoritative. Ashley smiled at him appreciatively. He'd learned a lot since the last time they were together.

They hadn't really talked yet, privately, about what had happened between them and what was happening now. Or what would happen in the future. But there was plenty of time for that.

In the subway, she'd told him about Corey, her

dreams and visions. He didn't think she was having a nervous breakdown.

And there was something she wanted to say, now. "Remember when we went to the Metropolitan Museum, and took all those paintings?"

He smiled. "We figured, since the rest of the world was gone, we might as well bring them back to the hotel and put them up there, where the few people left on earth could appreciate them."

"When we get back to New York," she said, "I think we should return them."

He understood what she was saying. "Yeah. I think you're right."

Cam joined them. "I was thinking," he said to Jake, "about those e-mail messages . . . I'd hoped that maybe some of them were coming from the aliens, but it looks like they all came from the group in California. Which makes me wonder, if possibly the alien life situation isn't as technologically advanced as ours is. Of course, the common belief, propagated by science fiction, naturally, is that other worlds would be more sophisticated and complex than our own . . ."

Ashley stepped back, to allow Cam some time to discuss this unintelligible stuff with Jake. She found herself beside David.

"I need a drink," David complained. "This plane better have bar service."

She took another couple of steps back, and walked alongside Martina. "How do you feel?" she asked her.

"Tired," Martina admitted, "but better than I've felt in a long time. Now that I know Rosa is okay." She smiled ruefully. "I realize everyone has lost loved ones, and I'm not saying that my loss was any worse than any one else's. But there's something about being an identical twin ... it's like you're two parts of the same person. I guess that's not so weird, I mean, we did come from the same egg. Anyway, I know everything's going to be all right now.''

"You do?''

Martina nodded. "I was able to bring her back here, even if it was just for a few hours, even if I had to take her place. So I know for sure now that she exists. They all exist.''

"Did you get any special information from your sister? Like, do you know why we're here?''

"No,'' Martina said. "She doesn't know anything. But she's hopeful now too. She thinks it's going to be okay. Only we're the ones who have to make it okay. They can't do anything.''

"You sound like you're still in contact with her,'' Ashley said. "Can you feel her now?''

"I can always feel her,'' Martina said simply.

They were walking on expressways, around empty cars and buses, under signs that pointed to exit ramps. Now the words on the exit signs were indicating different airlines. Ashley saw Air France, Air Italia, Aeroflot ... she wondered if, all over the world, people like them, people still on earth, were gathering, determined to find a way to bring all the others back home.

Ashley found herself walking with Donna and Travis now.

"Travis, I'm curious,'' she said. "Why did you decide to come with us? I know, you're going to be our leader,'' she added hastily after Martina gave her a look. "But why did you give up being the Community leader?''

"Because they were getting pathetic," Travis said. "I couldn't lead them, they didn't want to do anything. They're lazy. They don't deserve a leader."

He was so arrogant, Ashley thought with distaste. But she didn't let that show. They depended on him to get them all to California. But once they were there . . . She moved on quickly, till she reached Jake, and took his hand. He smiled, but his eyes were worried.

She wanted to tell him that it would be okay, that once they were safely landed in California, he'd be able to resume his role. But now Travis and Donna were right behind them, and she couldn't say anything.

No, that wasn't quite right. There was something she could say, something anyone could overhear and she wouldn't care. "I love you," she told him.

"I love *you*," he replied.

Love. The word reverberated in her mind. All kinds of love. Love between twins, between friends, between lovers. She thought about the love Corey had shown her back in the old days, the love that was propelling her to seek a way to rescue Corey.

It was all they had, this love, whatever kind of love they were feeling. But this love was what would save them.

All of them.

From the journal of Jake Robbins:
   We're sitting on this plane, heading to California.
Everyone else is sleeping. Ashley's head is on my
shoulder.

I can't see Travis, but I assume he's not sleeping. I can't sleep. Knowing Travis is up there in the cockpit, with our lives in his hands, makes me too queasy.

I don't know what we'll find in California. We don't know how many people are there, what they know, what they've been doing. Everything is so uncertain. I need to be strong, for Ashley, for everyone.

The plane ran into some turbulence. Jake's stomach lurched, and his grip on Ashley's hand tightened. He didn't wake her, though, and then the flight was calm again. He went back to his journal.

I don't trust Travis. But at least I know we're heading in the right direction.

Discover the exciting conclusion of the
LAST ON EARTH trilogy in

BOOK THREE: THE RETURN

*coming from Avon Books
in February 1999*

---

the flight had been calm for over an hour. Maybe that was why the sudden, brief shudder produced a muffled scream from the rear. Jake looked over his shoulder at the frightened girl who gripped the hand of an unsmiling boy.

"You okay, Shalini?"

Alex answered for her. "First time on a plane." His expression made it clear that they didn't want to be bothered, so Jake turned to the girl who sat next to him.

He knew for a fact that this wasn't *her* first plane ride. Ashley had been an almost supermodel in her former life, and she'd flown all over the world for fashion shows and photo shoots. A little turbulence wouldn't bother her. In fact, she had slept right through it.

Now the plane was steady again. Jake addressed the passenger across the aisle. "Looks like Travis really knows how to handle a plane."

The small, pale boy didn't look up from his laptop.

"Cam?"

With a show of reluctance, the boy tore his eyes from the screen. "What?"

"I was just saying, Travis didn't lie about knowing how to fly a plane."

Cam nodded and turned back to his computer.

Jake shifted restlessly in his seat. He'd flown before, many times. Every summer, before it happened, he and his family had flown to Florida to have a vacation with his grandparents at their condo in Boca Raton. But he'd never had to sit still for this long before. How long was a flight to California, anyway? Five hours? Or would it take longer in a small plane like this?

He was bored. He tried again to start a conversation with Cam. "What are you doing?"

It was a moment before Cam replied. "Checking out the chat rooms on the West Coast."

"Find anyone?"

"No, not yet."

"You hear from the group in Los Angeles again?"

"Yeah, they're meeting us at LAX."

"What's LAX?"

"The airport."

"Oh." Jake stretched his neck to get a look at Cam's screen. "Hey, how did you get online? There's no phone on this plane, is there?"

"Remote," Cam replied shortly.

"Huh?"

"It's a remote device, like a cordless phone. It's too complicated to explain."

Jake didn't take offense at the comment. They all acknowledged Cam as the only one among them who was truly computer literate and understood the intricacies of technology. As long as he took care of that, he was excused for his social inadequacies.

Funny, Jake had always thought of himself as

pretty inadequate in that regard. Before, back in the senior class at Madison High, he was considered something of a loner. He'd tried not to get too involved in other people's lives. Now, with only twenty-five people left on earth to communicate with, he'd somehow become a leader.

But at this moment, no one seemed to be in need of a leader's companionship. Gazing around, he saw Kesha with her eyes closed, apparently sleeping. In front of her, Martina was engaged in what appeared to be a very private conversation with David. Interesting, considering the fact that Martina hated David's guts for having broken the heart of her twin sister, Rosa, just last summer.

Jake had to smile to himself. Just a couple of months ago, he wouldn't have been privy to gossip like that. Now they all seemed to know everything about each other.

So . . . Alex, Shalini, Cam, Kesha, Martina, David, Ashley . . . Who was left? Donna had to be up front in the cockpit, taking great pride in the fact that her boyfriend was flying the plane. Jake was forced to return to the mode of communication he'd relied on before he became, for better or worse, a leader of a small group of survivors.

He pulled his journal from his backpack, and opened it to the last entry, composed just a couple of hours ago.

So now we're on our way to California to meet with this group who survived the Disappearance. At least we can be pretty sure they'll be on our side, and we have an idea of what we're up against. Sort of.

Beside him, Ashley stirred. As he looked at her beautiful face, she opened her eyes and smiled. "Hi," she murmured.

"Hi," he replied. "Hungry?"

"No. Thirsty." She snuggled against his shoulder. "Ring for the flight attendant and get me a Diet Coke."

"Very funny," Jake replied. His hand caressed the soft fuzz on her head. "Your hair's growing."

"Mm," she said drowsily. "That's what hair does." Then she was asleep again.

With a sigh, Jake went back to his journal.

> I'm trying to imagine what the others are doing back at the Community. Getting nuts, probably. Travis was the only element holding them together. keeping them relatively normal.

As much as he'd disliked Travis's form of totalitarian government, it had kept the party animals in check. By now, they were probably engaged in a nonstop orgy of sex, drugs, and rock and roll. Of the fifteen kids who had stayed behind in New York, not one of them had any real leadership qualities in Jake's opinion. After the Disappearance—D-day, as they called it now—Travis, as senior class president, had automatically been handed the role of presiding over the twenty-five survivors.

Jake didn't have any problem with this at the time. He certainly had no aspirations to lead the group himself. But when Travis turned into a dictator, and refused to consider the possibility that the world they'd known was not past recovery, Jake had been pressured into leading an alternative group on a mission to discover what really happened.

And now they knew—sort of. At least, they could assume that the population of the world, the citizens of Earth, were still in existence—in some other place. In some other form.

As for Travis, he was with them now. Jake kept telling himself that was good. The more the merrier, safety in numbers, united we stand and all that. But in the back of his mind, a question remained, and it itched like a mosquito bite. Who was their real leader?

He didn't want to think about this now, so he returned to the journal and tried to think of something new and original to write.

I wonder what these guys in California are like. It's weird, we're just getting used to thinking of ourselves as the last on Earth, and it turns out we're not. Cam hasn't found out too much about them. We have no idea how many of them there are. We don't know why they survived. Of course, we don't know why we survived either. They probably don't know any more than we do.

He read his words over. Then he added "Or maybe they do." And how would that affect the balance of power, he wondered.

He frowned. Why was he torturing himself with questions he couldn't possibly answer? He needed to take a minute to count his blessings.

He was alive. He was whole and intact and he still had his feet firmly planted on Planet Earth.

Well, figuratively speaking, he amended that, as he glanced out the window at the clouds floating beneath them. Most important, the person he loved was alive, whole, and sitting beside him.

As if on cue, Ashley opened her eyes. "Hello again," he said.

She straightened up in her seat. "How long was I sleeping?" she asked.

"Long enough for me to miss you," he said in his deepest, most poetic voice.

She grinned. "Oh, that's excellent. Keep talking that way and I just might think you're coming on to me."

"And you just might be right," he said.

Ashley laughed out loud. "We sound like a very stupid teen movie," she pointed out to him.

"That's because we're two very stupid teens," he replied.

She punched him lightly. "Speak for yourself." She stretched and moved her head from side to side as if to shake the sleep out. "I had the most amazing dream. It was so real."

"About what?"

"Corey."

That wasn't the answer he wanted to hear, but he went along with it. "What about Corey?"

"The usual. I could see him, I could hear his voice. In the dream, I was trying to let him know we're coming to save him, but he couldn't hear me. Just like the other times."

"Of course, this time was just a dream," Jake noted. "It wasn't like before, when you were having those visions on TV."

"It seemed just as real," Ashley said thoughtfully. "And if he can get inside my television set, why wouldn't he be able to get inside my head?"

Jake didn't reply. He couldn't say he was crazy about the idea of another man getting inside Ashley's head. But Ashley went on talking, not sensing his discomfort.

"Corey's an incredible person, Jake. If anyone could get into my head, he could. I can't wait for you to know him."

Jake had already heard many, many times about the kind of person Corey was. He knew that the fashion photographer had been a special and protective friend to Ashley. That still didn't explain why he was appearing to her in visions and dreams.

"You never saw anyone else in those TV visions, did you?" he asked her. "Like your mother, for example. She must be there, too, wherever Corey is."

"No, but she doesn't have Corey's spiritual strength, his ability to connect," Ashley told him. "She could barely get through to me when we were standing side by side! Corey . . . it was like he *knew* me, better than I knew myself. We had this bond, you know? He could see beyond all the hype and the glamour and all that supermodel crap. He knew what was real. I could communicate with Corey in a way I'd never communicated with anyone in my life."

She didn't add "until I met you." He tried not to accept the twinge of jealousy that tugged at his heart, but it was there. That little green-eyed monster had taken up permanent residence.

Ashley had assured him that her relationship with Corey had never been romantic. From what Jake understood, Corey had been more of a father figure, a big brother, something like that. In his mind, he envisioned a much older man, balding and paunchy, with a jovial Santa Claus air. Or maybe he was young and handsome, but effeminate, flamboyant, and probably gay. Certainly not the kind of guy Jake would ever consider to be a threat.

But even so, the idea that anyone else—young, old, gay, straight, male, or female—could be closer to Ashley than he was . . .

Suddenly the plane lurched. There was a familiar squeal from the rear. Then the plane began to bounce, hard, and even the more experienced fliers began to take notice.

Ashley slipped her hand into Jake's. "I hate this," she murmured.

"It's just an air pocket," Jake said, but his own stomach was flip-flopping as the plane continued to bounce. It felt like they were riding in an old car and there were massive potholes on the road.

The plan dropped, and now even Cam looked up from the computer. Jake shifted in his seat and saw that Shalini was sobbing softly and Alex was deathly pale. The plane plunged again—A thousand feet? Two thousand feet? Martina had a rosary in her hand and her lips moved. Even Kesha, who prided herself on her strength and composure and lack of fear, was gripping the arm rests of her seat so tightly that her knuckles had turned white.

Jake knew he should do something, say something, try to calm them all down. But he was scared, too, and he didn't know what to say. Now the plane was rocking back and forth, like a tiny flimsy boat on an immense, angry sea.

Through an intercom, the disembodied voice of their pilot cut the tension. "Sorry, folks, I couldn't talk to you sooner because I was trying to navigate us out of this turbulence. It looks like we're going to have a few more minutes of this. In these small planes, you feel everything. But there's nothing to worry about, it's all normal, and everything's fine up here. So take a deep breath, try to relax, and I'll get us through it as quickly as I can.''

Travis's calm voice had the effect of a verbal tranquilizer. Jake could hear the sighs of relief as everyone released their fear and tension. And Travis was true to his word. Within minutes, the turbulence disappeared.

Donna appeared from behind the curtain. ''Is everyone okay?'' she asked anxiously.

There was a general murmur of assent. Donna smiled happily, her eyes shining with pride. ''Isn't he wonderful?'' she asked simply. Then she disappeared back behind the curtain.

Ashley was smiling. ''Now, *that's* the face of a woman in love.''

Jake turned to her. ''Is *this* the face of a woman in love?''

Ashley rolled her eyes. ''Oh, Jake, have a little faith.''

She was right. Why did he have to be so damned insecure? Ashley loved him as much as he loved her, and he had to stop questioning it.

Love wasn't the only thing that made him feel insecure. Travis . . . just now he'd sounded really good, totally confident and in control. And everyone seemed to take comfort in his words and to believe them. They were trusting him with their lives. Which was as it should be, Jake supposed. Didn't people always want to trust the pilot of their plane?

But he couldn't help wondering if this trust

would extend beyond their flight to California. Which, in Jake's opinion, was *not* as it should be.

Kesha tried to be discreet as she let out her breath once the plane became steady again. She didn't want her fear to be apparent to the others on the plane. And she certainly didn't want anyone to think that the cessation of her fear had anything to do with Travis.

She really had to let go of that old rivalry. Just because Travis had beaten her in the election for senior class president last spring was no reason to hold a grudge, especially given their current circumstances. That would be just too juvenile, especially for someone like Kesha Greene. Kesha Greene had a reputation. She hoped nobody had noticed how scared she was. Were they all talking about her now?

She leaned back in her seat, and allowed herself to eavesdrop surreptitiously on the conversation going on in the seats behind her.

David Chu, the Don Juan of Madison High, was speaking. "Look, Martina, I didn't want to hurt Rosa. I just wasn't ready to make a commitment."

"Did you tell her you loved her?" Martina wanted to know.

"Maybe," David allowed. "Probably. Yeah, sure, I said that. But it doesn't mean anything."

"It meant something to Rosa."

"Yeah, well . . . I didn't know she was taking it so seriously."

"Did she mean anything to you at all?"

"Of course she did!"

At that point, Kesha took out the Walkman she'd brought on board and firmly clamped the headset to her ears. She hit the play button and let the happy reggae rhythms block out any further conversation.

That exchange between Martina and David . . . it was not only uninteresting, it was incomprehensible. She couldn't understand how or why any woman could fall in love with David Chu. Okay, in all objectivity, she had to acknowledge that he was incredibly handsome in a conventional sort of way. But he was also shallow, superficial, and as far as she could tell, intellectually limited. Not to mention morally and ethically challenged.

She hadn't really known Rosa, except for a brief time when her spirit had taken over Martina's body back in Central Park. But she knew Martina, and since they were identical twins, she had to assume they were similar in nature. She couldn't imagine someone as smart as Martina falling for a guy like David.

She tilted her seat back. Now she had a glimpse of Shalini and Alex. What a pair *they* made. Alex was your basic leather-jacket-rebel-without-a-cause, the son of Russian immigrants. Shalini was the shy, demure daughter of traditional Indian parents who still believed in male domination and arranged marriages. What could those two possibly have in common?

Then there were Travis and Donna. That was the most difficult relationship in the world for her to understand. Donna was her best friend; they'd been pals for years. How she could fall madly in love with a plastic political beast like Travis was beyond Kesha.

But then, most of the relationships she observed were beyond her comprehension. Jet set supermodel Ashley and moody Jake from Queens—where did that come from?

It dawned on her that the only other person sitting alone on the plane was Cam. But that wasn't surprising. Cam was a tekkie, a nerd, a computer junkie whose socks never matched. People like Cam were never in couples.

And what about people like Kesha herself? She'd always been reasonably popular; she'd always had friends. But she'd never been in love, and no one had ever been in love with her. It never used to bother her much. She figured she'd meet Mister Right someday. He'd be strong, determined, a brother, of course, someone who wouldn't be intimidated or put off by an energetic, assertive young woman who refused to conform to stereotypes of femininity. She thought she'd find him in college or out in the real world. Maybe they'd be working side by side in the inner city.

She couldn't count on that anymore. As far as she knew, at the moment there were only thirteen potential Mister Rights on the face of the Earth, and none of them came close to her ideal. To be honest, she knew she wasn't their ideal either. Maybe in California . . .

Her thoughts were disturbed by Travis's voice. "We'll be landing in about twenty minutes," he intoned. "Please put your seat backs in upright positions, return tray tables, and fasten your seatbelts."

Pompous ass, Kesha thought. If they weren't landing for twenty minutes, why did they have to put themselves in landing position *now*?

People were responding. Across the aisle, she saw Martina take out a compact and check herself in the mirror. She could hear Cam closing his computer. But there was no expectant buzz or sense of anticipation in the cabin. The silence was heavy.

Kesha broke it. "How many people are going to be there?"

"I don't know," Cam replied. "The person I've been e-mailing with, he never said."

"He? You know it's a he?"

"No," Cam acknowledged. "I don't know anything about him. Or her."

"Or it." That came from Alex.

"What do you mean, 'it'?" Jake asked.

"How do we know this isn't some kind of scam?" Alex fired back. "We could be walking into an alien trap."

Martina spoke. "If aliens had been communicating with Cam, they wouldn't need to lure us to Los Angeles. They could have taken us from wherever we were, just like they took everyone else."

"Yeah, well, whatever," Alex said. "All I know is, we're landing in Los Angeles, we're totally defenseless, and we don't know what's waiting for us."

"You got another option?" Martina asked.

Jake joined in the discussion. "Yeah, instead of complaining, why don't you present an idea, Alex?"

"Because none of you want to hear my ideas," Alex shot back.

"Because your ideas always suck," David said.

"Would you all please shut up!" Ashley burst out. "I'm feeling nervous enough already."

Maybe she had good reason to be, Kesha thought as the plane began its descent. Maybe they all did.